their bodies trembling with the heat of the
argument.

"I'll yell at anyone I please, and right now it
pleases me to yell at a little prima donna who is
running from her own talent."

Ayn told herself it was anger drawing them
together, but the passion in Gerick's blue eyes
belied her excuse. She refused to back down. "*I*
made you what you are today."

"*You* made me?" He threw his head back and
laughed ominously. "Ha!"

"If I hadn't walked out on you . . ."

"If *you* hadn't walked out on *me!* I made you
leave. Just like now, you don't have the courage
to . . ."

"You want courage," she shouted. "I'll show you
courage!" She drew her hand back, but Gerick's
strong fingers curled around her wrist.

RHETT DANIELS

tries to incorporate her desire to write with her love
of the performing arts. A seasoned movie buff, she
believes that the motion pictures of the thirties and
forties capture romance with a flair, a quality she
tries to portray in her own novels. Although she has
traveled throughout the United States, Rhett has
settled in Tulsa, Oklahoma.

Dear Reader,

Silhouette Special Editions are an exciting new line of contemporary romances from Silhouette Books. Special Editions are written specifically for our readers who want a story with heightened romantic tension.

Special Editions have all the elements you've enjoyed in Silhouette Romances and *more*. These stories concentrate on romance in a longer, more realistic and sophisticated way, and they feature greater sensual detail.

I hope you enjoy this book and all the wonderful romances from Silhouette.

Karen Solem
Editor-in-Chief
Silhouette Books

RHETT DANIELS
Overtures of the Heart

Silhouette Special Edition

Published by Silhouette Books New York

America's Publisher of Contemporary Romance

SILHOUETTE BOOKS, a Division of Simon & Schuster, Inc.
1230 Avenue of the Americas, New York, N.Y. 10020

ISBN: 0-671-53684-2

First Silhouette Books printing August, 1984

10 9 8 7 6 5 4 3 2 1

America's Publisher of Contemporary Romance

Printed in the U.S.A.

BC91

To Ada and Margaret for believing in me when I didn't.
Without your help this would be an unfinished symphony.

And a special thanks to Kathy for giving up her summer.

Overtures of the Heart

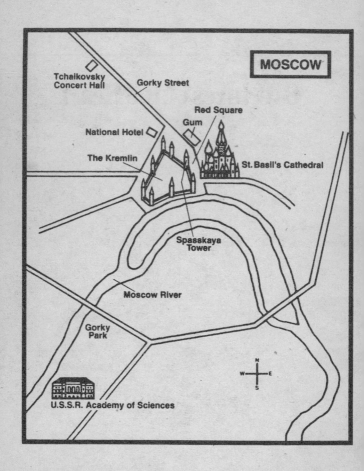

Chapter One

$\mathcal{A}$nd there he is," Jonathan announced, pride swelling his barrel chest. He stood and drew a wide arc with his arm, motioning toward the entrance of the restaurant.

Jonathan loves to be dramatic, Ayn thought, smiling at the white-haired man she'd come to think of as her father. She watched the half dozen people around the table as they tried to see between the potted plants lining the top of their booth.

"Who's here?" Ayn asked, deciding she should play along with the conductor's theatrics.

Jonathan cleared his throat. "Ladies and gentlemen of the board, and Ayn"—he nodded her way—"I have secured for the Interurban Symphonic Orchestra's next season the world's foremost violin virtuoso!"

Ayn felt the happiness suddenly drain from her. No, she thought as her hand gripped the delicate stem of the goblet in front of her, it can't be. Please, tell me it's Miguel Julianno. It has to be! Then she noticed the dark-haired woman across the table from her. Mrs. Bradley's face lit up as she recognized the man approaching them. Ayn didn't turn to look. She didn't have to. She knew Miguel would not cause a blushing glow on any woman's face.

It's the Great Gerick Grier, she thought, remembering how the press had referred to him in the last few years. Not only was he billed as a consummate concert violinist, surpassing even Heifetz, but as a jet-setter and one of the most eligible bachelors in America.

How could sweet old Jonathan have done this to her? She bit her lower lip and swirled the amber-colored liquid against the side of her wine glass. Ayn knew she was wrong to feel ungrateful. Most associate musical directors would give anything to work with such a performer as Gerick. It was her own fault. She kept her secret far too well. Jonathan didn't know about the life she'd shared with Gerick. No one knew, except the two of them.

Had it only been ten years? It seemed as though it was just the day before, and yet the changes they'd gone through made it seem an entire lifetime ago. They met when they were both students at Juilliard, so young and so ambitious. She closed her eyes against the memories playing in her mind. Her thoughts drifted to a time when no one outside the music industry cared who they were, or what they did. Even among their own, the names Ayn Remington and Gerick Grier were only spoken on the lips of a few who said they were newcomers to be watched.

That was when they had shared everything, an exuberance for music, an apartment too small for two people, and an overwhelming love for each other. Theirs wasn't the normal type of love Ayn had seen other couples fall into. No, their love was different. It was special. The love they had known didn't breed familiarity and habits, or settle into dull routines. Ayn and Gerick had shared a delicate blend of affection rarely experienced. It was a blend of light wispy heights like a Mozart sonata and soulfully deep grandeur as only Beethoven dared to obtain. Looking back, she often wondered if they had been fools, daring to believe they could live that marvelous mixture of emotions.

Ayn blinked back a quiet tear. How could something so beautiful, so full-bodied and complete wither and die?

From the booth behind her, Ayn heard the crack as one hand slapped a palm. Instantly the room thundered with applause. The private club and restaurant catered to the elite of the music world, and Ayn had never known anyone to receive an ovation at the Metronome. Sensing the warmth of a stare, Ayn glanced up to see Jonathan glaring down at her. It was then she realized she was the only one in the restaurant who wasn't standing and applauding.

If Jonathan could somehow understand the agony he was causing her, Ayn thought, then she wouldn't have to offer him an apologetic smile. She stood to join the others and hoped she'd kept the pain from showing on her face. Another look at Jonathan told

her she'd succeeded. Staunch as he was, if Jonathan
had any idea of her inner torment, he'd comfort her
in that portly manner he'd perfected. But, she'd
masked her feelings well—too well, perhaps. When
had she learned to rein her outward emotions so
callously? Apparently Jonathan's constant reminder
had finally been absorbed. "Control, Ayn, control!
It's the key to conducting an orchestra."

Suddenly, from a few feet behind her Gerick
spoke. "Enough! Please, enough!"

The crowd ignored him, but Ayn couldn't. The
resonant sound of his voice broke her facade. An
awful knot formed from the emptiness inside her and
her brown eyes brimmed with a glistening remem-
brance of Gerick and her.

"Control, Ayn," she whispered to herself. You're
a professional! You can make a hundred musicians
play together as one; surely you can handle one man.
She breathed deeply, then exhaled slowly and
turned. It was time to face her past.

The gasp that formed in her throat could hardly be
contained. She couldn't help but stare. The years
had been good to Gerick. If possible, he had become
even better looking. The dark blue suit complemented his tall frame, and beneath the gabardine
coat was a light blue shirt. In keeping with the
roguish reputation he'd developed over the past ten
years, Gerick wore no tie. The french collar of his
shirt was unbuttoned and offered a teasing glimpse
of his tanned chest.

It was a chest that seemed too broad and muscular
for a musician. Even though concert violinists are
known for their powerful arms because they pour
their whole body into their instruments, Gerick's

physique appeared far too large. He was six foot three and always seemed to overpower his small Guarneri violin when he placed it beneath his chin and poised the bow above the strings.

His black hair was swept away from his face, and although he was only in his early thirties, there was a trace of silver that lent him an air of elegance. The tiny fingers of silver wove into the dark hair at his sideburns, but the touch that photographers loved to capture was the streak of silver on his right temple. Somehow the shimmering against the black waves of hair added a compelling aura of mystery.

Ayn's gaze rested on his mouth and she wondered if his lips were still as soft and warm as they had once been. From the shadow beneath his high Scottish forehead shone his bright blue eyes. Eyes so clear Ayn thought she could see through them, but one deep look left her shivering from his intense stare.

She watched as he moved among the crowd, acknowledging his friends and accepting the adulation of his peers with a graciousness Ayn envied. Finally he held up his hands to signal an end. He bowed slightly in one direction, then in another, and offered a muttered, "Thank you."

The commotion faded and Gerick strode gracefully toward their booth. Ayn noticed that his gaze quickly encompassed the group of people, but he avoided looking directly at her. The anticipation felt sour inside her. How would he handle their reunion? Did he hold a resentment, perhaps even hate her, or could he possibly still feel a loving bond between them? Ayn had seen his anger lash out at others and she knew she would be no match for him if he decided to confront her.

"Gerick," Jonathan said, taking a step toward the younger man and offering his hand.

Gerick accepted the handshake. "I'm honored to be here." He glanced over his shoulder. "This is quite a reception you've planned. I'm overwhelmed."

Jonathan threw back his head and laughed; then he patted Gerick's wide shoulders. "I planned nothing. That was totally spontaneous. Surely you know how your fans adore you? Why, you have people coming to concerts who have never been interested in classical music."

"Yes, but these people are musicians, people I work with every day. . . ."

Ayn was amazed at his apparent humility. Perhaps the years had not changed him as much as she had thought.

Jonathan leaned closer to Gerick, but Ayn heard his teasing comment. "Maybe if you spent more time among the people of your trade instead of dancing till dawn at the discos, then you'd know your fellow musicians are the first to appreciate great talent."

Gerick's laugh was low and rumbling. It had been so long since Ayn had heard the music of his laugh, and it tickled a memory deep inside her.

"Just tell me this, Jonathan. Have I acquired the world's best conductor, or a new father?"

Jonathan ran a slender hand through his white hair. "Both," he said with a laugh. "Now, come on, let me introduce you to the board members."

Ayn stiffened as she realized that within seconds she would have to speak to him. She was seated on the outside edge of the booth and Gerick moved to stand beside her. His nearness shattered her composure. She became so engrossed in the alluring fragrance of his cologne that it took her a moment to realize the strange sensation she felt was caused by Gerick's hand at the small of her back.

He leaned forward to shake Mr. Bradley's hand and her eyes widened in disbelief as he used her body for support. She started to pull away from him, but his hand cupped her waist and held her tight. Part of her rebelled at his possessiveness and part of her reveled at the sentiments aroused by his touch.

Jonathan's voice invaded her senses again. "And I'm sure you've heard of my associate music director, Ayn Remington."

"Yes," Gerick said, turning to face her, "we're old . . . friends."

Ayn was afraid he was going to say they were old lovers, but when their eyes met she knew he would never again say anything to deliberately hurt her. The years seemed to melt away as he held her gaze with his. For a moment she felt like the young girl who used to look at Gerick and not believe she was fortunate enough to have won his love. She used to ask herself how she could possibly deserve such a magnificent person as he was. It had amazed her when Gerick confessed having the same doubts about his own worthiness of her love.

Gerick released his hold on her waist and took her hand in both of his. "How good it is to see you again, Ayn."

She nodded through her daze and gave a half smile. Why wouldn't her voice come?

"Well," Jonathan said, rubbing his hands together. "Since you two are old friends, I'll pull up a chair for you here between Ayn and me."

"Don't bother," Gerick said, lifting his hand to motion her back into the booth. "There's plenty of room on the seat next to Ayn."

Jonathan took his place in the chair at the head of the table and everyone sat down. Ayn tried to give Gerick as much space as possible, but Mr. Johnson's plump body on her other side wouldn't budge. Gerick pressed his left side against her and the heat from his body danced through her.

Ayn found it hard to concentrate on the anxious chatter around her. She was too aware of Gerick next to her and the desire within her that raged like a fire that could not be controlled. How could she let him affect her so? Had she no power over her emotions? No, not where Gerick was involved.

She had always known it would be this way and had purposely made her exit from parties and benefits before he arrived. Once she had fought her fear and gone to see him perform. Even in her seat in the back row of the concert hall she was moved by his presence. Now, fate had put them not only in the same room, but so close that his thigh continually rubbed her leg.

Against her will, his touch took her thoughts on a journey back in time to a small apartment in Greenwich Village. She remembered the last time they had been together . . .

. . . A kiss, feather soft and warm. He's home, she thought before blinking awake. The dim light of dawn peeking through the window spoke to her of the hour. Morning again. Where had he been? She knew what she felt for Gerick was true love, for nothing else could hurt so completely. Her heart was splintering into a thousand pieces. She ached to ask him what was keeping him away from her every night until almost daylight, but, afraid of the answer, she never asked the question.

She smiled up at Gerick. The smile he gave back was empty. Closing her eyes, she hoped he hadn't seen the disappointment in them. It was becoming harder and harder to hide her feelings. When she opened her eyes again, she tried to let the love in her heart, not the worry in her mind, show on her face. Gerick stared at her and she noticed his normally sparkling eyes were a pale blue. He was tired, almost worn beyond emotion.

"Hold me, Gerick," she pleaded as he buried his face in the soft curls of her brown hair. "Please, just hold me."

She wound her arms around the broad expanse of his shoulders and pulled him close. Something was wrong, terribly wrong. It was something that hadn't been evident before. Releasing him, Ayn pushed Gerick onto his back and stared at his face. Oh God, she thought, he knows! But how could he possibly know already? She hadn't been offered the position until the night before and, as usual for the past three weeks, he had been gone when she'd arrived at the apartment.

She ran her finger down his cheek. He caught her wrist with his strong grip, then turned his face to her and kissed the tips of her fingers. As though the tension inside them exploded at the same time, they lunged for each other.

Gerick gathered her to him. Heat radiated between their naked bodies as he molded his length to hers. The muscled band of his arms drew her nearer, as though they could become one. The coarse dark hair of his chest caused her breasts to tingle as he moved his body against hers.

His lips settled on hers in a firm kiss that demanded a response from her. Ayn arched her body into the rhythm of his and moaned at the song of joy he was creating within her. The passion of his kiss almost took her breath away.

Gerick's hand sought her breast and he massaged her peak to a firmness that struck a sensitive chord within her. Ayn drew in air quickly, and the nibble at Gerick's lip froze into a gentle bite. When her breath returned, she released her hold on him and Gerick abandoned her mouth.

As he trailed moist kisses down her neck, desire quaked through her veins, threatening to erupt. He kissed the curve of her breast, and a sensual need spread through her limbs. She became aware that he was as aroused as she was.

Ayn fanned her fingers against the bareness of his chest. Her hands followed the hardness of his flesh down his sides. His taut stomach muscles jerked at her light touch and she shuddered at the strength of his need. His mouth was on hers again, crushing her lips with his urgency.

"Oh, Ayn," he breathed into her. "I love you."

The hairs of his thighs felt rough against the smoothness of hers as she slid her leg over his. Ayn pressed his pulsing ache against hers and suddenly Gerick's hand covered her stimulating fingers. His breath came in ragged gasps that matched her own as he shifted positions and crushed her more fully onto the bed. Gerick took total control as his body rose above hers.

Ayn longed to be fulfilled, and the yearning caused her to draw in her breath when he gently prepared her to accept his love. She met the tempo of his cadence and was surprised at the suddenness of his movements when he eased into her. She moaned and closed her eyes with a sigh. His strong arms slid beneath her shoulders as he lifted her slightly and cushioned her against his entry. She hungered for the completeness they should know together, and answered his craving. He seemed to pierce her soul with each thrust.

She called his name almost before she realized it, and he growled his response, then took her mouth captive. The raw desire of his probing tongue seemed to draw her onto a higher plane. She could do nothing but allow her whole body to join him. Gerick knew the moment and he lovingly shared the experience with her.

Then they lay cocooned together in the warmth of the sensations they'd created. Ayn held to him desperately, but she knew she only held him physically. His soul had somehow escaped her. The timing was all wrong for them. Why had the position in San Francisco been offered the previous day? A month earlier she would never have considered leaving Gerick, or worse, asking him to follow her. That was before he'd grown so distant. Lately she'd found herself silently asking what she'd done wrong. The only answer was her career. It was taking off ahead of Gerick's.

In spite of how he had fought it, Ayn knew Gerick felt a slight resentment because she'd come from a socially prominent family. He, on the other hand, had been raised by a widowed mother and he had had to struggle up from the Lower East Side. Ayn liked his mother. She was a good woman, but a woman who'd had to be concerned with making a living for the two of them and couldn't afford music lessons for her son.

Ayn snuggled into the protective curl of Gerick's arm. They were so different, as varied as Strauss and Bach. Was it only their passion for music that they had in common? Strange, music had brought them together, and that day it threatened to tear them apart. She forgot the old questions as new ones haunted her. Could she deny the dream she'd sought all her life, and yet, could she deny her love for Gerick? . . .

". . . Don't you agree, Ayn?" The woman's voice was a shrill interruption to Ayn's thoughts.

"Pardon me," Ayn said, shaking her head. "Did you say something?"

Mrs. Bradley lifted her nose slightly higher. "I asked if you agreed, since you read over all the new material for the orchestra."

"I'm sorry," Ayn said, studying the woman's tautly drawn face. "My mind was somewhere else. You shouldn't need my opinion, though, Mrs. Bradley. You're as much an expert on the new trends as I am."

The woman beamed her delight and Ayn relaxed momentarily.

Gerick tuned out everyone around him and stared at Ayn's profile. She had grown into a beautiful woman. Her beauty was the natural type. She rarely used makeup, although he had seen her made up for the lights and cameras when she conducted, and she was stunning.

He wanted to hold her again as he had done the last morning they were together. She had been so responsive, almost urgent in her desire for him. As one, they had loved, and fallen fulfilled into each other's arms.

He silently scolded himself, sure he was the weakest man on earth for loving her so, but the memory was still so real. Every nuance haunted him, like the texture of Ayn's hair when he rumpled it lovingly while cradling her in the crook of his arm . . .

. . . Turning his head, he stared out the window of their second-story apartment. The rumor was true; Ayn had been recommended for the position in San Francisco. He'd seen the indecision written on her face. Gerick closed his eyes, thinking of the opportunity it would be for her. He couldn't hold her back, but could he possibly let her go? She was everything he'd ever wanted, everything. Without Ayn he'd be incomplete as a person, more music machine than man.

Ayn stirred in his arm and rubbed her soft cheek against his bare chest. He turned back to her and kissed the top of her head. Dark lashes fluttered and she opened her brown eyes, giving him a smile. For a moment they regained the silent language that exists between lovers; then he saw her large eyes cloud with doubt and he knew reality had claimed them again.

One of them had to say it, to start it. Someone had to be brave enough to begin the end. He rubbed the side of her jaw with his thumb. My sweet little Ayn, you'll never be able to do it, will you? Leaning forward, he kissed her gently. He wanted to brand his kiss on her tender lips so she would always carry the mark of being his, but it was too late for that.

When he drew away, Gerick saw the trace of a tear on her cheek, but she turned her head quickly and buried her face against the side of his neck. He didn't lift her chin to face him as he knew he should. The sight of Ayn crying would be more than he could take.

He spoke suddenly. "Ayn, I've been doing a lot of thinking."

"You've certainly had enough time lately for thinking."

Her voice was weak, but it cut through him. He wanted to tell her the truth, that he had to take the night job as janitor at the school to help support them. No, that would make her feel guilty and he had already hurt her enough. And, he thought sadly, the hurting isn't over.

It was best this way. If she was angry with him, then she would have the courage to take the job and move to San Francisco without him.

He propped himself up on one elbow. "And just what is that supposed to mean?"

"You're gone every night." She wrapped the blanket over her shoulder. "Your studies are falling. I haven't seen or heard you practice in weeks and . . ." She paused and looked away.

"And you? You're feeling cheated, right?"

"Yes," she defended, her bottom lip beginning to tremble. "Yes, I am."

He rolled away from her and was out of the bed in an instant. "Did you ever stop to think that you were being selfish?"

The pain in her eyes made Gerick turn away. He took his trousers from the chair where he'd laid them and pulled them on. He wished they could be transported into the future to a time when all this was over. A time when the pain had become a soft hurt in their memories and they could meet again, as friends.

"Gerick, we've forgotten how to talk to each other. Can't we try to talk this out? Wouldn't it be worth the effort?"

Damn! Why was she being so understanding? He turned back to face her. "Talk! Well, I'll tell you one thing. Gerick Grier doesn't have to answer to anyone, least of all *you*. If you don't like it, then you know where the door is."

He grabbed her red kimono from the chair and threw it at her. Ayn rose to her knees and snatched the robe in midair. She stuck her chin out with determination. "Maybe I'll do just that!"

Gerick sat in the chair and propped his elbows on the overstuffed arms. He forced himself to remain relaxed, in control of his emotions and Ayn's. "Fine," he said, keeping his voice flat, without inflection. "Whatever pleases you."

In a flash of red she rushed into the bathroom and slammed the door behind her.

Gerick slumped against the back of the wingback chair. He hated what he had just done and he was overcome with revulsion. The dim light of a snowy dawn crept into the room and it seemed to touch everything that was Ayn. His hand dropped to rest on the arm of the chair and he glanced down at the small table beside him.

A narrow strip of sepia-colored paper caught his

eye. Slowly he reached down and picked up the pictures. He stared at the tiny set of four photos and wished the color were more true so he could see the rich brown of her hair and eyes. He had watched her sleeping so many times, her hair like a mahogany fan against the pillow. No picture could capture the way the sun danced through her shoulder-length mane, streaking the strands with gold.

He laughed quietly as he thought of how self-conscious she was of her smile. No one could convince her that her lovely smile was not too large. He had told her several times that it was perfect, but she never believed him. He looked at the next frame. That was the look he loved the most: her non-smile, when she was holding back, trying not to smile, and her dimples would show up better than ever. She had that rare face that could accept dimples without making her look childish.

God, he was going to miss her, but all he could give her was four pictures for a quarter at Coney Island. Nothing was going to seem right without her to share it with. Nothing would matter anymore. No, his music would matter, as it always had. He would devote everything to his music and she would do the same. They both had a second love to fall back on and they would both survive.

He stood and walked to the window. Why had he met her at this point in their lives? All he could do for her was slow her down at this point. Gerick balled his fist and drew his arm back. He didn't realize she'd entered the room until she screamed.

"Not your hand!" she pleaded as he slammed his palm against the windowsill with an oath.

He was too numb to feel the pain and too embarrassed by his foolish gesture to face her. Ayn moved so quietly that he flinched when she slipped her arms around his chest. The sweet smell of her perfume drifted to him as she rested her head against his back.

"Oh, Gerick. I'm sor—"

"Ayn," he interrupted, still staring straight ahead. "I think we've said enough."

"But, Gerick, I love—"

"No, Ayn!" He had to stop her. "You're taking up too much of my time." She stiffened, and he took a long breath before he delivered the final blow that would send her out the door forever. "Ayn, you're hurting my career. I don't want to compete with you anymore."

She released her hold on him, and he watched her reflection in the windowpane as she moved away. Refusing to give in, he dropped his gaze to the floor, knowing one look, one word, would send them rushing back to each other. He heard her pause at the door; then, in a silent instant, the room was empty. Empty as his life would be from then on.

He lifted his gaze back to the window and watched the street below. Ayn was descending from the stoop. Her black coat made her a dark figure against the gray-white of the snow. He knew she'd slip in and gather her things, but he wouldn't be there.

Ayn hesitated, and Gerick pressed his palms against the windowpane. "Turn around, Ayn," he whispered. "Oh God, Ayn, come back."

Slowly, she started walking again. Wind whipped the snow furiously and tiny flakes swirled around her small body. As she walked away from their life together, Gerick wished he was caressing her like the wind. . . .

"Gerick," Jonathan said, moving his hand in front of his face. "You were a thousand miles away."

"Not that far really," Gerick said, smiling. He turned and draped an arm over Jonathan's shoulders. "I'm very honored by the offer to join the Interurban Symphonic Orchestra."

Ayn sighed with relief. Why had Gerick been staring at her for so long? Everyone at the table had noticed. Thank goodness Jonathan had finally distracted him.

"Oh, Ayn," Mrs. Bradley said, waving her jeweled fingers at her. "We were visiting friends out of town last week, and they took George and me to see the road show production of *Rainbow*. Of course I told them I'd seen it when it was the hottest show on Broadway."

"Thank you." Ayn couldn't keep her pride from showing. "I hope they enjoyed it."

"Oh, they did. Your score is superb."

Mr. Andrews shook his finger at her. "My wife cries every time she hears the album. Isn't that right, dear?"

The thin woman seated next to Mr. Johnson nodded. "Your music really does set the mood for the entire show. It's as if the actors are taking direction from your score."

Ayn started to speak, but Mrs. Bradley cut her off. "I can hardly wait to see the movie. When will it be out?"

"I don't believe they're even starting production for another four months, maybe around Christmas."

"Too bad you couldn't work on the movie, too," Mr. Bradley added.

"I could have, but Jonathan was already too kind to have granted me the sabbatical to compose the original. Besides, I don't think more time off would be fair to him." She flattened her hand and encompassed the table of people. "Or to you. Least of all, to our patrons."

Ayn refrained from mentioning that Jonathan's heart condition probably couldn't take the added strain. Only she, Jonathan and the doctors were aware of his health problem. The proud old conductor had not wanted to let anyone know, but the physicians' insistence that Jonathan slow down had made it necessary to tell Ayn. That was the reason she'd cut her three-year sabbatical in half and returned to the ISO full time a year ago.

As associate director, Ayn had always assumed more responsibility than her apprenticeship required, so it was quite easy for her to accept the balance of Jonathan's workload. It had been obvious to everyone from the first that the master was grooming his protégée for a musical directorship with one of America's "Big Six" orchestras. Her takeover of every detail, except the actual conducting, seemed a natural part of that training.

Ayn glanced at Jonathan, who, with his white hair and dark eyes, bore a striking resemblance to Toscanini. She knew that Jonathan, like the legendary Italian conductor, had not planned to retire until he was almost ninety. His dream had seemed shattered a year ago, but as Jonathan often stressed to anyone who would listen, to have a career in music, one had to remain flexible but determined.

The intimacy of Gerick's breath near her ear was felt by Ayn before he spoke. "Tell me, Ms. Remington, what made you want to break from classical to Broadway musicals? I mean, the critics, the public and even our own kind are very skeptical of that type of change. It could have ruined your career."

Her answer was automatic, a speech she'd given many times. "Every conductor reads music and studies its origins. Some fool themselves into believing they understand exactly what it consists of, but a piece can't possibly become real until you've tried it for yourself. Music is like love: until you've lived it and felt it yourself, you can't understand the depth involved. I had to take the chance to gain the experience, to try and comprehend every style of orchestration."

"Your success is being compared to that of Leonard Bernstein with *West Side Story*. That's quite an accomplishment," Gerick said. Ayn searched his eyes wanting desperately to believe that he believed in her.

"Well, I for one am proud of you," Jonathan said with a shake of his head. "Damn proud! It takes a lot of courage to try a different form of music just for the learning experience."

Again he gave a firm nod, and a shock of hair fell across his forehead as it often did when he was conducting. "Ayn, like myself, has learned to trust in chance. If we don't take chances we never realize our potential or our limits. Of course, as we've all discovered, Ayn has no limits."

Mrs. Bradley cleared her throat in the same irritating manner she used every time she was about to drop a bomb in the conversation. "Ayn may not have any limits to her abilities, but her career is certainly limited. You will have to admit, Ayn, your lack of European exposure is not good."

Ayn had learned to ignore similar comments from Mrs. Bradley and other musical snobs who still believed that everything worthwhile in the world of music came from Europe. She knew most of the influential people behind America's orchestras were of the opinion that conductors who received their training and directing expertise in Europe were omniscient, or at least they presented a more glamorous image of the knowledge they had.

It had not been Ayn's intention to buck the system or to be a rebel; it just happened. After her term in San Francisco she went to study in Austria, and like all young conductors, she hoped a symphony on the Continent would offer her a position. It only took a month to realize the training she'd received in America was as good if not better, and since the United States was where she really wanted to conduct, she returned home.

Several friends who played in some of the "Big Six" orchestras shook their heads in disbelief. She was breaking the rules; her career was doomed. They swore there wouldn't be any way for her to gain acceptance by the major cities that made up the six—Boston, Chicago, Cleveland, Los Angeles, New York and Philadelphia—but Ayn held her ground. She kept remembering the one rule that overrode the politics and prejudice: talent can't be denied. Ayn didn't think of herself as another Toscanini, but she did recognize that what she did possess was a very unique gift that music lovers were ready to hear.

She relaxed against the back of the booth, not bothering to defend herself against Mrs. Bradley's comment. The older woman was the only dissenting member on the board, and Jonathan had asked Ayn to allow him the privilege of rebuttal, but before he could speak, Gerick interrupted.

"I must have misunderstood you, Mrs. Bradley. It sounded as though you were criticizing the very ideals that the orchestra was founded on."

Ayn lifted her hand to signal Gerick to stop. "Please, it's not necessary to—"

"No," Gerick said, taking her hand in his and lowering it to the table. "It is necessary. I think this whole question of European credentials is ridiculous."

Several seconds of Gerick's debate were lost to Ayn as she tried to ignore the way he was still clasping her hand in his. Her thoughts tumbled incoherently over each other until she glanced at Gerick's face. Seeing the unmoving determination etched on his angular features, her thoughts collected. He was not defending Ayn the woman he once loved, but Ayn the conductor whose cause was one he believed in. His touch had sent swells of heat radiating through her, but Gerick was unaffected by his familiar caress.

Until that moment she had not realized that a small hope had existed in the back of her mind. A hope that Gerick still held at least a degree of love for her. His obvious absence of emotion made it clear to Ayn that he might as well be holding an inanimate object for all he cared. She blinked slowly. How could she work with him when his every look or touch had her responding like a woman in love for the first time? She sobered as a thought invaded her. In Jonathan's absence she'd be Gerick's boss, and she couldn't even look him in the eye.

Sometime while Ayn was absorbed in her doubts, Jonathan had assumed the monologue from Gerick. An intimidated Mrs. Bradley sat back quietly as Jonathan finished with his typical exaggerated expressions. A tense silence settled momentarily over the table; then Mrs. Bradley's husband stood suddenly.

"Jonathan, I think this calls for a toast. Would you propose a toast to our great luck at obtaining these two young, extraordinary people."

Everyone stood instantly. Gerick's arm circled Ayn's waist when she stood. A gesture which to the others seemed gentlemanly, but which to Ayn was quite disturbing.

Jonathan held his glass high. "To Ayn Remington and Gerick Grier, whose names are destined to become legends in the world of music. May the union of these two talents bring us the best season ever."

The tinkle of glass as everyone saluted them sent a shiver down Ayn's spine. One thought dominated her. This "union," as Jonathan called it, was never going to work.

Chapter Two

*A*yn, wait," Gerick said, catching up with her. "Judging by the way you ran out of that restaurant, I'd say you were trying to avoid me."

She kept walking. "I am trying to avoid you. Excuse me, I have an appointment." She hurried to become part of the herd of people crossing Fifth Avenue. To her dismay, Gerick ran with her.

As they stepped onto the opposite curb, he grabbed her arm and pulled her around to face him. The anger in his cool blue eyes made her wish she hadn't been so honest with him.

"Don't I deserve at least the same courtesy you'd give a stranger?" he asked.

"You want a quarter for a cup of coffee?" she asked, purposely giving him a blank stare. The effort was wasted. He didn't get mad; instead he smiled.

"I'm glad to see you haven't changed much."

She softened and stared at a crack in the sidewalk.

"That's just it, Gerick. I have changed, and so have you." She looked him squarely in the eye and immediately regretted the action. Ignoring the ache in her heart, she continued, "I don't think we should discuss anything except business. We need to keep this relationship on a totally professional basis."

He surveyed her as though he were seeing her for the first time. "So, who said this isn't business?" he asked, his features hardening again.

Ayn felt her cheeks flush with color. She nodded. "Okay, what is it?"

His sparkling blue eyes darkened with his answer. "I'd like to take you out tonight."

Ayn's eyes widened. "I thought you said this was business?"

He took hold of her other arm, forcing her to face him squarely. "We need to talk, Ayn. We can't keep up this facade that nothing has ever happened between us."

She looked away from him quickly, hoping he hadn't seen the hurt in her eyes. "I guess you're right," she said softly.

"Good!" He released her. "Once we clear the air, we'll be able to get on with this 'professional relationship,' as you refer to it."

Ayn withdrew a small gold case from her clutch bag. "Here's my card. My home address is on it."

"Well, well, we are being professional, aren't we?" he teased, glancing at the embossed card. A low whistle escaped his pursed lips. "Nice address."

"I believe in going first class." She smiled, then paled when she saw Gerick's face grow sad. Her mind raced, wondering what she'd said wrong.

"I've asked myself many times if that was part of

the reason you left. I never was classy enough for you, was I?"

His question stunned her beyond words for an instant; then, before she could deny the accusation, he turned and disappeared into the crowd.

"Gerick," she called, trying to follow him. "Gerick, wait!"

His height allowed her to pick him out in the throng. He stopped and glanced over his shoulder at her.

"What do you mean, *I* left you?" She pointed to herself, then to him. *"You* made me leave!"

He winked and saluted her. "See you at nine." Then he was gone again.

Ayn fluffed the assortment of throw pillows on both sofas for the fifth time. She started again for the glass coffee table to recheck the arrangement of plump pink roses and lilacs; then she stopped. Why was she so nervous? It was only Gerick. Her laugh was soft and delicate like the fragrance of the freshly cut flowers. Only Gerick! She'd seen women nearly faint from a brief encounter with him. A smile or a handshake could reduce the most sophisticated woman to childlike giggles.

Catching her reflection in the mirrored wall behind the baby grand, Ayn moved closer. Maybe she should have worn the red sequined tunic and black velvet slacks. No, she thought, shaking her brown hair into looser curls, that outfit looked too sexy and tonight that wasn't required.

She smoothed the pleats of her white dress and adjusted the metallic belt that matched her shoes.

As she gently finger-combed her hair, she noticed her hands were shaking. She hadn't been this nervous since she won the Franklin Foundation Award for musical achievement.

The door chimes sounded and she froze. If she hadn't felt her heart beating a staccato rhythm against her chest, Ayn would have sworn her heart was in her throat. She tried to swallow and found the effort difficult. Finally she pulled herself from her trance and moved toward the door, stopping momentarily at a small basket of dried flowers and brightly colored ribbons. The wicker basket hung suspended on a spring from the vaulted ceiling, and as she gave it a lucky tug she remembered Gerick had given it to her on their first Easter. She had replaced the ribbons, but the basket had gone to every home with her over the years. The chimes sounded anxious when they echoed again, and she hurried to answer.

"As usual," she said, opening the double doors, "you're right on time . . ." Her words trailed to nothing as she saw him. She had been too stunned that afternoon to see anything except her painful memories, but alone together, his presence overpowered her.

The three-piece suit of black pinstripe emphasized his wide shoulders. Gerick's hard, lean body was evident in the perfect fit of the suit. Tiny lines of silver threaded through the dark material and mirrored the contrast of silver and black in his thick hair. Beneath the tailored vest he wore a pearl gray silk shirt. His eyes were like the mirrored surface of a lake on a winter's morn.

Her voice was hardly more than a whisper. "Come in."

As he strode past her the heavy scent of his cologne brought back a flood of remembrances. Not of particular days, but moments. Moments filled with a joy she had forgotten could exist. She squeezed her eyes closed, thinking she couldn't go through with it. When she opened her eyes, Ayn started to ask him to leave, but the sight of his tall frame standing next to her lucky basket created a feeling of déjà vu. It seemed as though he'd always been there, as if he belonged there.

Gerick fingered a ribbon as he looked around the room. "Congratulations, I didn't think it could be done."

"What?" she asked, moving past him into the room.

"I didn't think it was possible to make one of these posh, high-rise apartments look like a home."

She nodded her thanks, glancing at the shell pink and beige decor.

"This room is you. Totally feminine, but alluring."

She smiled, not daring to look him in the eye. "Thank you. Would you like a drink, or something?"

"No, but I would like to . . ." He stepped toward her in a quick movement and Ayn gasped, moving back. He pulled up suddenly, his look indignant. "I would like to see the view from your picture window," he finished.

Ayn felt the color rise to her cheeks. She was acting like a fool. Where was Ayn Remington, the conductor? Why couldn't she treat him like any other member of the orchestra?

He continued staring at the twinkling New York skyline. "I frightened you a moment ago, didn't I? Are you that afraid of my touch, Ayn?"

"No," she answered, sounding more firm than she thought possible.

He turned to face her, his stare like frozen chips of blue ice. "You forget, Ayn, I know when you're lying."

"Then you know that when I said this was a good idea, I was lying." She glanced at his chiseled face and was immediately transfixed by his riveting blue stare. Though she didn't move, Ayn felt as if the distance between them had vanished. Why hadn't he looked at her this way on that winter morning? If he had, she never would have left, no matter how horribly his words tore through her.

"Neither of us is fool enough to believe that this was a good idea, but it is necessary."

Panic rose inside her. She wasn't ready to discuss their past. Until that afternoon she had thought she was over the pain and grief, but the instant she saw him she knew she could never be totally over Gerick. She had buried his memory so deep, it had only surfaced occasionally. When it did she hid it beneath the only other love she'd ever known—her music.

"Ah," he said, stepping to the wall, which held dozens of plaques and trophies. "Quite impressive."

"Thank you," she said, glad the subject had been changed. "I imagine the walls of your home are filled three times more than mine are. Of course, since your house is one of the world's best-kept secrets, who's to say what it looks like?"

He lifted his eyebrow and grinned. "Nice bit of

publicity, don't you think? International playboy who is always seen at the right place, at the right time, with the right people. My social life is an open book, but alas . . ." He touched the back of his hand to his forehead.

Ayn watched him, not daring to speak. She knew his humor was laced with anger and not mirth.

"Alas," he repeated, "no one has ever seen where I live. An aura of mystery, great gimmick, isn't it? How astute of the press to figure out my home must hold too many clues to the girl of my dreams who left me years ago."

Trying to ignore the hostile tone of his voice, Ayn sat on the piano bench and ran her fingers lightly over the keys.

He crossed his arms in front of him and leaned against the wall. "Imagine the headlines we'd create if they knew it was you, Ayn."

She stiffened, then pounded the keys. "Do you expect me to believe I'm the reason behind all this secrecy concerning your house? Nonsense! It's just like you said, Gerick; it's a publicity stunt."

"Don't worry, Ayn, I won't tell, and naturally you wouldn't think of it. Would you?"

Ayn didn't answer; instead she stood and moved to stare, unseeing, out the window. All she could think of was her desire to have the evening over with. Rubbing her temple, she wondered if she was going to spend the next seven or eight months wishing each day would end so she could start preparing for her next confrontation with him. She turned suddenly. "Gerick, I think—"

He had already directed his attention back to the awards and he lifted his hand to cut her off. Shaking his head with approval, he read from a large silver-and-wood plaque. "One of the ten outstanding women of the year, *A Better Life* magazine." He moved to the next one and tapped the gold plate. "Look here, we both made *Current*'s list of most-admired people last year. The first time in the magazine's fifty-year history that two people from the world of music have made the list. Too bad neither of us could break our previous engagements and attend the dinner."

"A couple of admirable cowards," she said without thinking.

The lines of Gerick's face hardened and the glazed blue ice of his gaze shattered with anger. She knew the fear in her own eyes was real as she silently pleaded with him. Appealing to the tender side of the man she used to know was the only defense she felt sure of at the time. He was determined to hurt her; she could see it. Gerick wanted revenge and she would be the loser in a word battle with him. Her emotions were riding too near the surface.

"I think we should go," he said suddenly, his face unchanged but his eyes full of melting warmth. "My driver is waiting."

Ayn nodded and scooped up her evening bag. She didn't breathe a sigh of relief that her sad-eyed look had worked. Ayn knew she hadn't won, she'd only delayed the inevitable.

They rode down on opposite sides of the elevator without speaking. Ayn tried to think of something to say, but she felt even small talk would somehow lead back to the subject she was trying to avoid. Gerick stared at her, and for the first time Ayn realized it took an awfully long time to descend twenty floors.

As the doorman ushered them into the warm September night, Ayn turned toward Gerick. "A limousine?"

He smiled. "I believe in going first class."

The remark made her want to explain everything. "Oh, Gerick, how could you think I would—"

"Not now, Ayn."

"Yes, now. I want you to understand. I was never the one who was ashamed of your upbringing."

"That's okay; your father was ashamed enough for both of you."

"That's not fair," she said, stopping. When he pulled up and turned to face her, she saw the vulnerability in his eyes and all resentment left her. She wanted to cradle his head against her breast and comfort him like a small child who had been hurt. Unable to act on her instinct, she whispered his name.

He placed his finger on her lips to quiet her. A tingle of pleasure licked through her veins at his touch.

"Sh-h-h," he breathed, then motioned to the chauffeur who was standing at attention by the open car door. "Later, Ayn. We'll discuss it later."

She bent and stepped into the elegant automobile, all too aware of Gerick's strong hand at her elbow guiding her inside. Again, they placed as much distance between themselves as possible.

When the door closed, Ayn felt trapped. Gerick made no move toward her, but his body was tense, like a cobra ready to spring at its victim. Soft music filtered to her as the car slipped into the traffic. Ayn studied the view outside her window as though she'd never seen the street before.

"Is something wrong?" Gerick asked.

His deep voice caused Ayn to start. "No!" He raised an eyebrow and stared at her in amusement. It wasn't fair that he could read her like a book. "I don't like that mood music," she snapped, desperate for something to say.

His broad chest rose with his laugh. "Have you become so prejudiced toward anything but classical music that you despise great Broadway melodies? I thought you were a devoted fan of Rodgers and Hammerstein?"

"I am, but that's not Rodgers and Hammerstein, it's . . ." Ayn stopped, recognizing the tune she'd written.

"It's by a young new composer/conductor," Gerick said, "and it's one of my favorites from *Rainbow*. The closing number of the second act, 'A Love That Will Not End.'"

Ayn blushed. She studied Gerick's knowing smile. He couldn't know that she had written the song thinking of him. She knew the feeling so well that she had even suggested some of the lyrics and the title, but there was no way he could have known it was autobiographical. She had told no one, except Jonathan, and even then she hadn't mentioned Gerick's name. Everyone loved the melody. Like "If Ever I Would Leave You" or "The Twelfth of Never," it had become linked with lovers. It was just a coincidence that he liked the song.

"You saw *Rainbow?*" she asked.

"Yes, and I was quite impressed with your score. You earned your Tony Award."

"Thank you," she said as the last refrains of the song died.

Gerick leaned forward and tapped the window that separated them from the driver. The glass slid down quietly. "The lady would prefer some classical music."

"Yes, sir," the chauffeur said as the glass silently closed again.

Strains of Prokofiev filled the compartment. "Sonata in D Major?" Ayn asked, leaning against the plush seat.

Gerick nodded, "The second movement."

The violin music seemed to carry her back in time. "I was there the night you won the world competition playing this piece. Your strings were like the laughter of a child. I was so proud of you." She turned to face him, realizing suddenly how open she'd been. Ayn sat up straight and stared ahead. She hadn't meant to let him know she ever thought about him.

"You were there?" he asked in surprise.

She shrugged. "I was in the neighborhood."

Gerick threw his head back and a deep laugh rolled from him. When he looked at her again, his eyes were dancing with the life Ayn used to see in them. "You just happened to be in Vienna?"

"I was studying in Salzburg," she answered flatly, not bothering to mention she had arranged her study to coincide with the competition.

His face dropped slightly. "Oh, yes, I remember reading that somewhere. So, it seems we have each been following the other's career from a very safe distance."

"Professional curiosity, I suppose," she said, shrugging again.

He nodded his agreement and they fell silent.

She hated the long moments of silence when he would just stare at her. Conscious of her every movement, Ayn touched the upholstery with nervous fingers. "Somehow I thought you'd have a sleek, fast sports car."

"As a matter of fact, I do, but this seemed more suitable for the occasion." His voice was a study in control, and she saw the splinters of ice had returned to his piercing blue eyes. "You have ridden in a limousine before, haven't you?"

"Of course. Though usually it is for our entourage, not just for two people on a date."

"Let's get one thing clear, Ayn. This is a business meeting, not a date."

She felt as if her heart had been ripped from her at the coldness of his words. Nothing could stop the mist that formed in her eyes as something inside her died. She turned away, pretending to stare out the window. Fighting for control, Ayn summoned every strength she had and found her voice. "I do realize this is strictly business, which is the *only* reason I accepted your invitation in the first place. 'Date' was a very poor choice of words. Forgive me."

"Certainly," he said softly.

The bright lights of the street projected Gerick's image on the dark interior windows. Ayn watched his profile without turning to face him. She ached to cup his face in her hands and run her thumbs over his prominent cheekbones. She wanted to feel the determined line of his jaw and gently kiss the strong, straight line of his nose. How appropriate that he should play classical music, when his features were so classic. Like a hero of ancient times, his look was powerful, almost immortal. A strand of black hair had fallen on his high forehead and she reached out to his reflection to smooth it away. The chill of the glass caused Ayn to draw her hand back. She sighed, realizing that the man beside her was equally as cold.

The car eased to a stop at the curb. Ayn turned and saw a long line of people waiting near the flashing neon entranceway to the disco.

"Oh, Gerick, no," she said, touching his arm.

He looked at her quickly; then his gaze lowered to her hand, which still held his arm. His stare seemed to burn her flesh and she released her hold.

"Please, Gerick, can't we go somewhere else? I'm not into this type of nightlife."

"You'll enjoy it once we're inside. The problem is getting through all these reporters and photographers."

The chauffeur opened Gerick's door and a thousand voices seemed to mix with the electronic music pouring from the converted theater building. Ayn cringed. Gerick started to climb out of the car, when a Rolls Royce screeched to a halt behind them.

Gerick muttered an oath under his breath and reached back to take Ayn's hand. "Come on, we're going to need each other's support to get through this one."

"Who is it?" she asked, sliding across the leather seat.

"Terra Spencer and her new beau," he answered, stepping from the limousine.

Ayn froze in the doorway of the car. Terra Spencer! At first the name only conjured up the face of a beautiful Broadway singer who was trying desperately to break into movies, but then Ayn realized why Gerick was so concerned. For the past six months he had been seen almost exclusively with Terra. Their picture was on the front page of every tabloid and their names were linked together in every gossip column.

Ayn hung back. She didn't like publicity, except when she was on the podium. Seeing that the reporters had gathered around the young starlet, Gerick jerked his head back and motioned Ayn out of the car. With a tug, he physically pulled her to her feet. She lost her balance and fell against his chest. The feel of the solid muscle beneath his shirt sent a wave of longing through Ayn. She wanted to slip her arms around him and hold him close as she once had. There was an ache deep inside her to hear the steady rhythm of his heartbeat as she lay with him, fulfilled and content.

The need churning inside her must have been evident on her face, for Gerick tilted her chin up to look at her. His clear blue gaze locked on her brown eyes. Gerick's stare was so intense that his eyes shimmered and they spoke of his desire without voicing a word. He lowered his head and Ayn quivered with the anticipation. Part of her said he wouldn't kiss her in front of all these people, but another part of her didn't care where they were, only that he feed the hunger he'd aroused within her.

Someone in the line of people waiting to go inside suddenly recognized Gerick and pointed him out. Before they could move, Gerick and Ayn were surrounded. Questions popped as quickly as flash-bulbs. There were shouts as Ayn felt herself being shoved and pushed. "Get a picture of all four of them," a man shouted.

Ayn tried to protest, but a rambunctious interviewer with a tape recorder slung over his shoulder tripped and slammed into her. She moaned as she fell against Gerick.

"No!" Gerick said loudly, then waved the crowd away. His arm circled her waist and he drew her close to him.

She melted against his taut limbs. Her body wanted to go limp in the safety of his embrace, but she maintained control and allowed him to maneuver them toward the car.

The whole scene had only taken a second, and the chauffeur was just closing the limousine's door when he saw them returning. He snapped to attention and swung the door open again. Their attempt to escape only fed the reporters' belief that this was the story of the week, and they continued their hounding questions. The sound of shutters clicking was maddening as microphones were continually shoved near their faces.

"Hey," one man drawled. "It's that lady conductor."

Ayn's name was echoed several times and the crowd seemed to grow even more persistent. Gerick used his body to shield her from the barrage until they finally reached the car again. As she started to climb into the limousine, a sweet voice called her name. Instinctively Ayn looked up. An explosion of light temporarily blinded her; then a streak of black flew past her face. She managed to focus well enough to see Gerick slap the strobe light from the young man's hand. Quickly, Gerick guided her inside their vehicle, then followed her in. The door slammed shut behind them and once again their world was quiet.

Faint murmurs could be heard from outside, and flashbulbs continued to light the darkness. Gerick leaned his back against the door, blocking the view of those trying to snap a candid shot through his window. Ayn fell against the seat, allowing a long sigh to escape her lips. She was surprised at how vulnerable and exposed she still felt.

Gerick glanced out the rear window. "We'll be out of here in a minute, as soon as my driver can get through the crowd."

Ayn put shaking fingers to her temples and tried to press the ache away. Suddenly the door next to her opened and a thirty-five-millimeter lens began winking furiously at her. Almost before she could react, Gerick lunged across her and pushed the intruder away. He closed the door and locked it.

The shock she had felt was lost in the warm sensation the touch of his body created. As Gerick slowly moved back he paused, their faces inches apart. She could read nothing in his clear blue eyes—except concern. Gradually his lips began to part and Ayn hoped the velvet softness of his kiss would become more than just a memory. Instead he spoke her name in a whisper that was hardly more than a breath. He eased back into his place against the door and gently pulled her with him.

She pressed her palms against the solid wall of his chest and wondered if she was doing the right thing. One quick look in Gerick's eyes told her it was the only thing to do. She rested her head on his shoulder and leaned against him.

The chauffeur burst into the car, took his place in the driver's seat and wheeled the automobile into the traffic. Ayn started to sit up, but Gerick's arms closed around her and held her close. The security of his arms erased the fear the mob had forced on her. She smiled, thinking how protected she felt now, wrapped in warmth like a Rachmaninoff rhapsody.

At the traffic light, the glass partition slid down and the chauffeur looked over his shoulder. "Where to, sir?"

"West Fifty-second Street. You know the place." The driver nodded and smiled.

"And," Gerick added, "take the long way . . . just in case any of those reporters try to follow us."

"Yes, sir," he answered. Then Ayn saw him wink at Gerick in the rearview mirror. She didn't believe Gerick any more than the chauffeur had, but she felt too good to say anything. She had missed being held like this.

They drove in silence through the theater district and up to Columbus Circle, then turned toward Central Park South. The multicolored lights fused with the sounds of the traffic and the people, creating a beautiful harmony.

"Someday I'm going to write a symphony that captures the feel of New York," Ayn said, then wondered why she'd admitted one of her deepest secret ambitions to Gerick. Actually, she'd completed the symphony, but she felt it needed polish and she wasn't ready to let anyone know, especially Gerick.

He smoothed her hair. "That would be a masterpiece. Gershwin tried with *Rhapsody in Blue,* but I think his theme was too broad."

Ayn sat up. "Oh, his theme was very clear; it was all American. It's mood, it's tempo, everything spoke of the people, the society. He knew it well, only—"

"But, genius as it was, he never seemed to pull it together, to make it one composition instead of four separate tunes."

Ayn blinked her surprise. "I can't believe you feel that way."

Gerick shrugged. "That's the way I hear it."

"So do I! But usually when I say so, people think I'm putting down Gershwin and I'm not. I adore his music, but I want to go one step further. I want to develop an American symphony around one city, one people, New York." She heard her voice become more excited with each word. When she finished, she felt as if she had been bubbling as she spoke.

Gerick's eyes grew distant, but he kept smiling. "Music is your life, isn't it?"

"Of course! It always has been. It will always . . ." She hesitated. He wasn't just talking about the surface of her life, he meant the entire core. Softly she completed the sentence. ". . . be an important part of my life. I can't picture my life without music in it, but there are other things equally as important that I would prefer not to live without. I'm sure you feel the same."

She hoped he wouldn't ask her what those other things were, for at the moment, staring into his blue eyes, she was afraid she'd answer that it was him. He knew they were both too weak emotionally, and he left the question unchallenged. His hand reached out to her and she placed her palm against his. Slowly his fingers laced through hers.

"We are a lot alike," he said, and gently squeezed her hand. "We meet on a common ground called music, but then we go our separate ways."

Still holding his hand, she relaxed against the seat. He wanted more from her than she had been willing to say. An admission of some sort, a statement of her feelings for him. If she only knew, but her feelings were so confused she couldn't admit them to herself, much less to him. She allowed her head to roll to the side and looked at Gerick's profile. Neither of them knew what they wanted; every time they started to talk, they ended up hurting each other.

"Speaking of music," Gerick said, interrupting her thoughts, "here we are."

The chauffeur eased the limousine to the curb and jumped out quickly while Ayn looked around, trying to place where they were. She knew she'd been in the block before, but almost too long ago to remember.

The door swung open. "West Fifty-second Street," the driver announced.

Gerick climbed out, then turned to help Ayn. She glanced up as she stepped from the car, and stopped.

"Oh, Gerick," she said, her voice brimming with tears of joy. "Roseland ballroom. You remembered."

He offered his arm to her, and she slipped her hand through to rest on his forearm. "I thought you might enjoy a step back in time. Only we won't have to live on peanut butter and jelly for two weeks to afford it this time."

Ayn laughed as they entered. "It was worth every

stale piece of bread for that one night of sheer romance."

"I don't know, I thought everything we did was pretty romantic, or were we just too young and too much in love?"

"Too young," she said, and looked at him. Their gaze met as it had on a starry night years ago. "And too much in love."

He patted her hand. "I wonder why your first love always happens when you're too young to appreciate it?"

Ayn shrugged and looked around for something to detour them from the collision course she knew their reminiscence would run. "Oh, look," she said, pointing to the display cases. "They still have Fred Astaire's and Joan Crawford's shoes."

He followed her lead and they moved on with small talk as they located a table, then sat back to enjoy the parade of people around them. Gerick pushed their chairs together and draped his arm over the back of hers. She leaned against him, wondering how long their stolen moment of happiness would last.

"You know, it's not that expensive to come here," Gerick said. "In fact, it's very reasonable." Ayn smiled at the feeling as his chest vibrated with a laugh. "We were just so damn poor it seemed like dinner at The Four Seasons to me."

"It didn't have to be so bad, you know?"

"Yes, if a certain Miss Park Avenue could have learned how to budget money."

She sat up suddenly and put her fist on her hip.

"Whoa," he said, tapping the end of her nose.

"I'm only teasing. I realize you had to have money to budget before you could come up with anything left over. A struggling student with a part-time job just didn't give a girl much to work with."

"We could have used the money my father allotted me," she said hesitantly.

Gerick sighed. "Will you never understand? I couldn't, Ayn, I just couldn't."

"It would have been so much easier if you would have at least let me contribute."

He leaned forward, resting his elbows on his knees. "I brought three things with me out of that tenement: a desire to be the best, at something; a secondhand violin in a cardboard case; and my self-respect. If I had allowed your father to support either of us it would have stripped me of what little self-esteem I had at the time."

Ayn stared into the endless blue of his eyes. "I'm sorry, I never meant to ask you to be less of a man than you are."

He took her hands in his. "You didn't. You always stood beside me, defending my stubborn pride, even to your father."

Ayn looked away, remembering how displeased her father had been at her choice of careers. Falling in love with a musician was the last straw for Bradford Remington. He thought they were both foolish children and told them so, many times.

"How is your father?" Gerick asked, touching her chin with his finger and turning her back to face him.

"He's fine."

"Still rich?"

"Yes," she answered with a soft laugh. "He's

finally accepted my career and we get along much better now."

"I heard he'd remarried, someone quite a bit younger than he is."

Ayn nodded. "He and Stacy seem perfectly content and the age difference doesn't bother me in the least. In fact, I rather like it. He's so busy keeping up with her that he doesn't have the time to try and run my life anymore."

"Good!"

"I was sorry to hear about your mother," Ayn said, touching Gerick's arm. He drew back, but his face never changed. Quickly she added, "She was a very special person. I really liked her."

"Thank you. She thought a lot of you, too. You should have heard the lecture I got when she found out I'd made you leave."

Ayn pointed an accusing finger at him. "So, you admit it. You made me leave; you left me no choice."

He shrugged. "I admit to nothing. I'll plead the Fifth Amendment."

"Seriously, Gerick, we do need to discuss it. After all, that was the purpose of the evening, wasn't it?"

Gerick leaned back and locked his fingers behind his head. He stared up at the swirling lights above the dance floor.

"Gerick."

"Listen!" he whispered, as "A String of Pearls" began on the downbeat. "Next to classical music, I believe I love the sound of the big bands best."

Ayn sighed. He wasn't ready to talk about their past, and she was glad. Gerick placed his hand on the top of her chair again and she leaned back into the curl of his arm. Closing her eyes, Ayn hoped they might be able to regain a few minutes of the sheer romance they'd known years before.

When she opened her eyes, the sounds and the location brought back another memory. "Remember old Rosy, who had the apartment below us, and her vintage collection of Benny Goodman? I swear, she must have had every album he recorded."

"And she loved to play them, loud, at night, about two A.M. Oh yes, I remember her well," he answered with a smile.

"She always loved to come here. I don't think she missed a single Wednesday night the entire time we were there."

"Our one night of sleep. Of course, I really didn't mind the other nights either. We usually found something to do if we couldn't go back to sleep."

Color rose to her face. She couldn't believe how often he'd made her blush in one day. During the ten years since they'd parted, no man had broken her exterior shell.

She looked away to the dance floor. "You don't suppose old Rosy might be here tonight, do you? I'd love to see her again."

"I doubt she'll be here on a Friday night. She probably has a date."

"True," Ayn said with a sigh. Then she sat up suddenly. "Look, I think that's her. Over there."

Gerick gave a quick glance into the crowd. "You must be mistaken."

"I'd recognize that carrot red hair anywhere. Oh, look, she sees us." Ayn lifted her hand and waved to the old woman.

"No," Gerick said, firmly gripping her wrist and pulling her hand down.

Ayn looked at him in shock, but he offered no explanation. Then she heard the familiar raspy voice and knew Gerick's action had come too late. Ayn stood and turned to greet her friend.

Rosy's round face was as well made up as it had been years earlier, and in the same style. Ayn gave a genuine smile as she opened her arms and welcomed the small woman.

"Ayn, Ayn! I can't believe my eyes," Rosy said in the heavy Irish accent she'd kept since her youth. "Lass, you make an old woman's heart happy." They separated and stood an arm's length away, admiring each other. "What a beauty you've become."

"Rosy, you haven't changed a bit. Still full of the old blarney."

"I swear by the saints above it's the truth. Ain't that right, Mr. Grier, she's a beauty?"

Ayn glanced over her shoulder at Gerick, who had moved to stand behind her. She thought she caught him motioning something to Rosy, but he stopped and smiled when he saw Ayn looking at him. She frowned and turned back to the short woman. "He's not that big of a star that you have to call him mister. We're old friends, remember? Gerick will be just fine."

Rosy nodded. "I know, he tells me that all the time, but I just can't break the habit. Like they say, you can't teach an old dog new tricks, and out of respect I call him—"

"Say, Rosy," Gerick interrupted. "Are you here with a date?"

The old woman grinned. "Naw, I don't like to dance more than two songs with any one man. I like to get around, you know."

"Well, then, if your card is not full, may I have this dance?" Gerick bowed low in a dramatic gesture.

Rosy covered her mouth with her handkerchief when she giggled. "For you, Mr. Grier, I'd throw the card away."

As Gerick moved around Ayn and took the woman's elbow, she wondered if it looked to anyone else as though he was rushing the sweet old woman away. Ayn sat and watched the short, red-haired woman being waltzed around the floor by the tall handsome man. She saw that others around the room had noticed Gerick's striking looks. Pride swelled within her; then she remembered how strange he'd acted about Rosy and felt confused again.

One band took a break, but the other band began a new song immediately. It was "Spanish Eyes" in a South American tempo. Gerick and Rosy struck a pose, then began to tango. Ayn smiled at their fun, but stopped, realizing she was feeling a tinge of jealousy for not being the one in his arms. She knew it wasn't against Rosy, but against Gerick for letting her leave him and for all the years they'd wasted.

Ayn motioned to the chair across from her when the dancers returned. "Won't you join us, please?"

Rosy gave a quick look at Gerick, then shook her head. "No, Ayn, another time. I've got men to meet. You wouldn't want me to disappoint all those lucky gents, would you?"

Ayn nodded her agreement as Rosy leaned over

and kissed her cheek. "It's so good to see the two of you together again," she whispered. When she straightened, the old woman smiled up at Gerick. "Thank you, Mr. Grier, for making me the envy of every woman here. Take care of our little Ayn." She shook a finger near his face. "And don't be such a damn fool this time. Hold on to her!"

Ayn laughed at Gerick's expression as he watched the old woman walk away. "I guess it's obvious who she likes," Ayn teased.

"And after all I've done for her, too."

"Do you still see her much? She acted like—"

"I'm in the old neighborhood a lot and we see each other now and then."

Ayn rested her chin on her hand as she leaned against the table. "I'd like to see the old place again. I wonder if that grouchy old super is still there? What was his name?"

"I don't remember, but he's gone anyway. The building has a new owner."

"Gerick," Ayn asked, glancing up at him, "why are you still standing?"

"Because—" He stopped, and as though it were on cue, the band struck the familiar chords of "Stardust." "They're playing our song." He held out his hand to her.

Ayn took his hand and allowed him to guide her to the dance floor. She whirled to face him and held her arms up and out as she tried to prepare her body for the feel of his arms sliding into position around her. Gerick was an elegant dancer. He held her right hand out from their bodies at just the correct height. The strong fingers of his right hand fanned across her back and waist, creating a burning sensation where they touched her. He uttered her name in a guttural growl and she looked up only to be trapped in his gaze. With a grace seemingly unnatural to a man of Gerick's height, they started to glide around the floor. He never let her look away from his piercing blue gaze—not that she had any desire to.

She was vaguely aware of the glittering chandeliers and streamers that swirled above them as they moved quickly around the room. Riveted to his stare, she was molded to his body as they turned and turned and turned. Her senses reeled as he pulled her deeper into a place where only the two of them and the music existed. It seemed as though her feet would actually leave the floor at times, as they spun into a surrealistic world of their own.

Chapter Three

*A*yn," he said, his voice almost a laugh. "Ayn, have you come down to earth yet?"

She still felt giddy and shook her head slightly. "What? Did you say something?"

"We're home, Ayn. If you'll give me your key, I'll unlock the door for you."

She rummaged in her bag automatically and tried not to think about here and now. It had been too wonderful. Their stolen moment had grown into hours. She held out her hand, the key resting in her palm. When Gerick took it from her she had to resist the urge to hold his hand.

A click sounded and he pushed the door open. "There," he announced as light from the hallway rushed into the room, then he stopped abruptly a few feet inside the door.

Ayn felt her mood begin to drop. She didn't want it to end. She couldn't say good-bye, not while the world seemed perfect.

"Since you seem to have forgotten your manners, I'll help you along. Yes, I'd love to come in for a nightcap."

Ayn smiled and walked into the apartment ahead of him. The door closed behind them, drowning the room in darkness again. She moved to the arc lamp by the picture window, but as her fingers found the switch, Gerick's hand closed over hers.

"Let's not spoil the mood," he said, and pulled her around to face him.

"Gerick, that was the nicest business meeting I've ever had."

He placed his hands on either side of her face. Long slender fingers fanned across her cheeks and he ran his thumb along her soft warm lips. She melted and revived instantly at his touch. Gerick's blue eyes caressed her as tenderly as his embrace. A look passed between them like the climax of Beethoven's Fifth Symphony. He lowered his head while gently drawing her to him. Ayn watched the sensual line of his lips as his mouth descended toward her. The moment seemed suspended in time and she moaned the agony of her anticipation.

Suddenly Ayn realized Gerick had stopped. Her anxious gaze searched his eyes and found a flicker of fear hidden deep in their brilliance. She understood. They were fast approaching the point from which they could only move forward. Once they declared their physical need still existed they would have to face their past as well as their future. They could not go back to their charade of being just friends. She shared his pain at the realization that one or both of them could possibly be hurt, terribly.

His eyes shimmered like a wet midnight as they darkened with his desire. "You're even more enticing in the moonlight."

They were bound together then, in that tiny split second which held so much power. It was like the thrill Ayn experienced each time she was about to bring a piece of music to life. There was that instant, that magic moment when nothing else was right except to begin. A fraction of a second later the magic would disappear. She felt it deep inside her; the moment was exactly right. Ayn stood on her tiptoes and stretched to meet him.

His hands slipped to her shoulders and his powerful grip lifted her quickly. She felt the faint touch of his lips on hers before he took her mouth with his urgent desire. He had total control of her body; even her breath seemed to have no will of its own. His kiss gave her life and she submitted to the longing he drew from her.

Ayn slid her hands over his muscled shoulders and arched closer to him. Their bodies responded with a natural rhythm that seemed to feed the fire raging inside her, out of control. Just when she thought he could demand nothing more from her with his intoxicating kiss, he increased the pressure of his need. Her heart beat with such a force it sounded like a double forte in her ears, and she felt as if the room were spinning around them.

When she realized Gerick had started to pull away, Ayn tried to lure him again with the intensity of her kiss.

"Oh, Ayn," he moaned before he invaded her

senses with renewed passion. Simultaneously they discovered every nuance a single kiss could contain; then he gently pulled away from her. He held her eyes with his as he lowered her to the floor. Sensing that her limbs were too weak to support her, Gerick's long fingers remained on her shoulders to steady her.

"Ayn," he started, then stopped as though he were lost in her stare. She was mesmerized by the longing that still burned in his eyes. In a moment quicker than a blink she watched his gaze reflect his mood change. "No!" he swore, and released her so suddenly she stumbled to regain her balance.

He turned and walked across the room in long, defiant strides.

"Gerick?" she questioned as she recovered from her shock.

He shook his head, still not turning to face her. "No, Ayn. It will never work. *Never!*" Then, as quickly as he'd reentered her life, he was gone.

Gerick gave the chauffeur a large tip and stepped from the limousine. Then the long, sleek car prowled off into the darkness. The soft purr of its motor faded into the distant voice of a guitar that was coming from a nearby coffeehouse. Alone with his thoughts, Gerick stood staring at the brownstone in front of him.

For the first time since he'd bought the building, it looked cold and uninviting. The music filtered through his thoughts and Gerick considered going to the café but he didn't move. He knew he was to blame for his own state of confusion and that he had to sort it out by himself.

Until that afternoon the place where he and Ayn had lived had held only memories, good memories. After being with her again, he realized it held a past which couldn't be recaptured. He had been content to live with the ghost of Ayn, but it wasn't enough anymore.

"You should be here with me tonight, Ayn," he said aloud. "This was our home. You belong here."

Removing his suit jacket, he slung it over his shoulder and started up the steps. When he turned the doorknob, a flood of remembrances washed over him. He never ceased to be amazed that they'd only been together one out of his thirty years, yet his entire world seemed to revolve around that fraction of his life. He paused and tried to shake her memory from his mind.

Quiet footsteps carried him across the entry hall, but as his hand touched the dark wood of the banister, the door to Rosy's apartment opened. He didn't want to talk about the evening, but he knew Rosy would want every intimate detail and she wouldn't let him rest until she got what she wanted.

Gerick turned to face her and tried not to smile at her fuzzy green slippers that peeked from beneath a matching floor-length robe. Her bright red hair made quite a contrast with the pink foam curlers that crowned her head in neat little rows.

"Hello, Rosy. Sorry if I disturbed you when I came in."

She slapped at the air. "Now Mr. Grier, you know nothing bothers me when I'm sleeping. I wasn't asleep, though; I was waiting up for you."

"Somehow I thought you might be," Gerick teased.

"I can see those wheels turning inside your head. You're thinking I'm going to stick my long Irish nose in your personal affairs and ask something—"

Gerick silenced her with a wave of his hand. "Yes. No. And because it won't be officially announced to the press until Monday."

Rosy crossed her arms over her chest and leaned against the doorframe. "And what were my questions?"

"Did the evening go well? Will Ayn be moving back in? And why didn't I tell you I'd finally decided to go with the orchestra?"

"Well, thank you, Mr. Grier, but believe it or not, I was not going to ask you any of those prying questions. As a matter of fact, the reason I stopped you is strictly business."

"What's wrong? Has something broken down?" he asked, starting toward her apartment.

"No, no, nothing like that." She frowned. "What on earth could go wrong? You just finished having the whole place renovated a couple of months ago."

"So what is it?"

"A Mr. Jonathan Eichman stopped by tonight. He asked me to give you these." She stepped back into her apartment, then reappeared with an armload of musical manuscripts.

"The scores. Great! I was wanting to go over them." Gerick moved quickly to relieve Rosy of the burden.

"Mr. Eichman also asked me to give you this." She pulled a small piece of paper from the pocket of her robe. "Some sort of map and directions, I believe. He said he'd be there by noon and hoped you could fit the weekend into your busy schedule."

Rosy's matter-of-fact tone brought an apology to Gerick's lips. "Thank you. And Rosy, I'm sorry if I offended you by thinking you'd be waiting up to ask me about Ayn."

She shrugged. "Don't worry about it. You just go on to bed and get a good night's sleep. It sounds as though you're going to be pretty tied up for the next two days."

Gerick nodded and started up the stairs with another muttered, "Thanks."

"Oh, I almost forgot," Rosy said, snapping her fingers. "As long as we're both up, there is one more thing. What are you doing home so early? Why aren't you still with Ayn?"

As Gerick turned to face her again, his "I knew it" smile met her ornery grin. He shook his head, then sat on the step. Rosy eased herself onto the bottom stair. She patted the spot next to him to show that he should set the scores down.

He looked at the older woman, not bothering to hide the sadness in his eyes. "I don't know the answers. I was asking myself the very same questions." He paused, watching Rosy carefully fold the jacket he'd dropped on top of the stack of music sheets. "At first it was a little rough, but from the time we arrived at Roseland to just a few minutes ago, everything went fine. No, better than fine, great."

"So," she asked, looking up at him, "what happened?"

"I called it off and walked out," he said, hardly believing his own words.

Rosy clicked her tongue against her teeth. "Still holding that old resentment."

Gerick leaned his elbows on the step behind him. He focused on his thoughts, then shook his head. "How can it be resentment? How can I possibly hold it against her for leaving? I wanted her to go; she had to try it on her own if we were to have any chance together."

"There's your answer, Mr. Grier, in what you just said."

He sat up. "What? I don't understand. What do you want me to admit?"

Rosy stood. "Gerick," she said softly, "you don't owe me an explanation, but you do owe yourself one."

He rested his elbows on his knees and stared at Rosy, allowing his emotions to war with his pride. Reluctantly the words formed. "We never had that chance together again because Ayn stayed away. She was supposed to come back, Rosy." He hung his head in his hands. "She was supposed to come back."

Ayn awoke with a start. She was thankful for whatever had brought her out of her nightmare, but what had she heard? She looked around her bedroom, which was a study in the various shades of rose. The colors ranged from the lightest mauve to the deepest wine. Nothing was out of place. Falling back against the plum pillows, Ayn made a face. Something was wrong, but she couldn't think clearly enough to recognize what it was.

With a gasp she sat up again. Gerick! She had been dreaming about him. Slowly her thoughts collected and the previous day's memories rushed back to her in an uncontrollable flood. She pulled the satin comforter up to her chin and stared straight ahead. It didn't really happen, she told herself as she began to sink beneath the protective coverlet. It was all a dream. If she closed her eyes and went back to sleep, when she woke up she wouldn't remember any of it.

She squeezed her eyes shut and held them closed against their will. Reluctantly she opened them again. She peeked out from her hiding place and immediately saw a large reproduction of Gerick's face smiling back at her from the night table. Throwing back the covers, she sat up and grabbed the booklet. It was the program from his first performance at Carnegie Hall. Ayn cradled it to her breast as she remembered she'd fallen asleep staring at it the night before.

Before she had time to speculate about their evening, the door chimes rang. She rose from the bed and grabbed her silk kimono from the upholstered parson's-style chair. She hurried from the bedroom realizing the chimes had been the sound that woke her.

When she reached the front door, Ayn looked through the peephole. Securing the sash of her robe, she smiled and opened the door. "Jonathan, what on earth are you doing here?"

With his usual flair, Jonathan burst into the room. A white paper sack dangled from his teeth and he was balancing several styrofoam cups in his hands. Steam curled from the tiny opening in the top of each cup. He dropped the sack onto the marble top of the wet bar. "I knew you'd be running late, so I brought breakfast."

Ayn counted the numerous cups as he deposited

them on the counter next to the sack. "Eight cups of coffee? Who else are you expecting?"

"Cute!" he snapped, reaching into the bag. "Six for me and two for you."

"Has anyone ever told you that much caffeine is bad for you?" Ayn ignored her own question and walked to the window. With a tug on the drawstring, the draperies parted and a Manhattan morning spilled into the living room. Ayn winced at the glare of sunlight on the glass and metal of the skyscrapers. "Goodness, Jonathan, what time is it anyway?"

"Seven."

"In the morning?" she asked, her voice rising to an unnaturally high pitch. "I'd heard there was a seven A.M., but I thought it was a nasty rumor. Good night, Jonathan, wake me at a decent hour."

"Now, now, none of that. You're late," he said, spreading a thick layer of cream cheese on a bagel.

"That's the second time you've said I was late. Late for what? We don't have a rehearsal today, and if we did, it certainly wouldn't be at this ridiculous hour."

"I should have known. A handsome man like Gerick Grier walks into your life and you forget about poor old Jonathan."

Ayn blanched at the mention of Gerick's name. She gripped the edge of the piano and eased herself onto the bench. "Jonathan, how could you have hired him without even consulting me first?"

"I wanted to surprise you; I wanted to surprise everyone! Besides, it was all so uncertain until the last minute. Did you see the faces of the board members when I announced he would be our guest soloist for the entire season? It was even better than I had imagined." He paused. "Ayn, are you all right?"

"Yes," she answered, glancing up and offering a smile to Jonathan's concerned look. "I'm just a little tired. I didn't get much sleep last night."

"I figured as much when Gerick said you'd spent the evening together. That's why I catered the breakfast." He left the bar and walked to her with a styrofoam cup in his hand. "Here, have a little of this. It's guaranteed to get your blood circulating."

Ayn automatically took the coffee from him; then her eyes widened in surprise. "You've already talked with Gerick this morning?"

"Yes, and if you don't start to hustle, he'll be there hours ahead of us."

Ayn held the warm cup against her temple and stared at the white-haired man in front of her. Her voice sounded as weary as she felt. "He'll be *where* hours ahead of us?"

"Nantucket, dear, remember?"

Ayn came to life with her embarrassment. "Oh, Jonathan, I'm sorry. I forgot about our trip completely. Forgive me?"

"Of course. Now, get a move on. We have a lot of work ahead of us." He moved back to the bar and began his third cup of coffee. "Gerick took the music with him so he'd have a little extra time to go over it."

Ayn shot to her feet. "You sent the scores with him!" Jonathan nodded in surprise. "All of them?" Ayn asked, almost shouting.

"Yes." He shrugged. "Ayn, he hasn't seen them

yet. We've studied them for more than a year; don't you think he deserves a few hours at least?"

Ayn blew at a stray lock of hair. "Yes" was all she could say. She didn't want to tell Jonathan that her composition was among the other orchestrations and that she didn't want Gerick to see her work—not until it was perfect. Another thought suddenly came to her and she tried to keep her voice calm. "Gerick's spending the weekend with us at Nantucket?"

"Yes. This is supposed to be a working weekend, and Gerick's part of us now."

Thoughts of being cooped up in Jonathan's beach house for three days with Gerick began to flash before her. She could see them bending over the same sheet music, deciding the various tempi side by side at the piano. More unnerving than that would be knowing he was in the room next to her, sleeping, alone. She shivered at the unbearable thoughts.

"Jonathan, would you mind terribly if I backed out on this trip?"

"This whole weekend was your idea, remember? 'Let's go up to the island and get away from the city noise,'" he mimicked. "'Somewhere we can work without being disturbed.'"

"I know, but I'm really tired." She saw the conductor's eyes blaze and quickly added, "I think I'm coming down with something."

"No, you're coming up with something. You're coming up to Nantucket. We have a season to plan."

She hated to whine, but it seemed the only tactic left. "Please, Jonathan."

"Gerick said you wouldn't come if he went along," Jonathan said, shaking his head.

Ayn slammed her palm on the bar. "He what?"

"He said something about you being too chicken to test your professionalism. I'm not sure what he meant by that."

Ayn turned and raced toward the bedroom. "I'll be packed and ready in five minutes," she called over her shoulder.

Chapter Four

*A*yn leaned on the rail of the ferry and smiled at the invigorating smell of the sea air. Jonathan stood beside her, staring across the Sound toward Nantucket Island. He clapped his hands together and Ayn prepared herself for the same mini-history course he gave her every time they visited his hideaway.

"You know, Ayn," he started, but she finished his sentence.

"This island was once the home of New England's largest whaling fleet. In the mid-1700s . . ." Ayn stopped, seeing a strange look on Jonathan's face.

He laughed. "I guess I have told you about the island several times. It's just so fascinating to me."

She gave a small smile and patted his arm. "If I didn't know better, I'd swear you were an old nautical man instead of the world's greatest conductor."

A long sigh rushed from him. "I'm afraid I've lost that title, if I ever had it."

"Don't be ridiculous," Ayn snapped, turning around to lean her back against the slick wood of the railing. "Jonathan, there's not a soul alive who can even come close to you."

He shook his head. "There's a whole new generation of musical directors out there, and the best of that lot is standing next to me. Throughout my forty years in music everyone who is anyone has somehow, somewhere passed through me. I have touched so many careers, but a talent like yours is something a conductor dreams of leaving his legacy to."

In that moment she realized that all of her awards combined could not compare with Jonathan's heartfelt praise. He had touted her to others, like the board members, but this was different. The master was admitting to the student that she had exceeded him. Ayn didn't fully agree with Jonathan, but it felt incredibly good to hear it.

"Oh, Jonathan," she breathed, "thank you."

"Ayn," he said softly, "I'm seriously considering retiring."

She turned to face him, trying to read the reason behind his statement, but his features gave no clue. Studying how the years had loosened his skin, then left it to draw into a fine network of character lines, she suddenly felt the bond between them grow stronger. He was her mentor, her teacher, her friend. She drew from the experience of his age, and he was renewed by the spirit of her youth. So often

Jonathan was the only person who understood her obsession with conducting. Theirs was a dream shared by a very few.

She wanted to say so much, but the only word that would form was, "Why?"

"There are still things I want to do that conducting full time puts limitations on. You of all people should realize that, Ayn. You've written your Broadway musical and I think you have finished your symphony, though you won't show it to me. Well, I have a few sonatas floating around inside me, and I'd like to try and give Bach a little competition too."

"Forgive me for saying so, but aren't you a little old to try and outdo Bach? After all, he had twenty-one children."

Laughter burst from him as he hugged her. "We're a good team, Ayn. You always know when and how to lighten the mood."

"I know you've always been thrilled with the *St. Matthew Passion* and you've wanted to create something similar, but its just like you said a minute ago: we're a good team. Why break up something that works?"

"We are good, but you have the potential to be great and you know it." He leaned on the rail. "Don't worry. It won't be for a year or so. The orchestra is getting so big now, we have to make our plans in advance and I just wanted to let you know."

"Well, you may say you're retiring from conducting, but I know you, Jonathan. These hands will never stop communicating the emotions of music." She clasped his hands in hers, then drew back suddenly. "Your hands are like ice! Are you all right?"

Jonathan quickly shoved his hands into the pockets of his windbreaker. "I'm fine. It's being compared with a composer like Bach; the thought is sacrilege. It makes my blood run cold."

Ayn tried to laugh with conviction, but she failed and they slipped into an uneasy silence. It was probably nothing, she told herself, but first thing Monday morning she was going to make an appointment for them to see his doctor. She watched the bow of the ferry slice through the Atlantic, sending small whitecapped waves into the blue-green sea.

Jonathan broke into her concerned thoughts with his question. "You're not happy that Gerick has joined us, are you?"

She shook her head.

"He mentioned you two were old friends, and yet I've never heard you even speak his name in all the time I've known you."

"We're not really old friends; we're acquaintances. We went to Juilliard together, that's all."

"You do realize how much this means to our company, don't you?"

"Of course, but—"

"Ayn, you know your idea for the cultural exchange with Russia? For months on end all I've got is red tape; then suddenly they hear we have Gerick Grier, and the State Department and Russia are finally sitting up and paying attention to the proposal. He's our—"

"Wait!" Ayn said, holding up her finger to interrupt. "How did they *hear* we have Gerick if it hasn't been announced yet? The press conference is scheduled for Monday, right?"

"You know how impossible it is to keep a secret in our business," he said with a wink.

She laughed. "You think we really needed him that bad?"

"He's almost as important to our orchestra as you were when I snatched you up. Although I will admit you were more receptive from the start. Honestly, it took forever to convince him we had the most to offer. I did everything but beg him, and I would have done that if I thought it would have helped."

Ayn slapped her palm on the rail. "You see, Jonathan, that's my point. Gerick is a star, almost a superstar, and we don't need that kind of flash trash in the world of serious music. He'll be temperamental and hard to work with."

"I'll admit he likes to spend his evenings in places I care little for and he's seen with the jet set, but his escapades have made him a household name. That type of publicity has brought more patrons to the arts. When people hear he's joined us, money will flow in like mad."

The shrill whistle of the boat blasted above them to signal they were approaching the island. Jonathan turned toward his car and offered his arm to Ayn. She fell in step beside him, hoping their discussion of Gerick was over.

"By the way, the morning gossip columnists were buzzing with a new tidbit."

Ayn knew he was baiting her, but asked anyway. "About what? Or should I say 'whom'?"

"Let's see if I can remember how it was worded. Something like this: What violin virtuoso struck a photographer at a disco last night trying to protect his new flame, a well-known female conductor?"

"He didn't hit the man. He just knocked the camera from his hand."

Jonathan opened the car door for her. "So," he said, faking his surprise. "It *was* you and Gerick."

Ayn rolled her eyes. "It was a business meeting," she defended.

Jonathan nodded. "Ayn, we don't need that kind of flash trash in serious music," he said, mimicking her own words as he closed the door.

Ayn watched him walk around the car to the driver's side.

"If I didn't like you so much," she said when he opened his door and seated himself behind the wheel, "I'd slap that silly grin right off your face."

He laughed. "That was a low blow, wasn't it?"

Ayn nodded, folding her arms.

"My point is, you are not being very fair to Gerick. I want you to give him the respect he deserves. He is a guest of the orchestra and will be treated as such."

"I'll try," she said as Jonathan started the engine. "For your sake. But it won't be easy."

"Why do I keep getting the impression there is a lot more here than meets the eye? I got the same tense feeling from Gerick when I talked to him. Ayn, is there something between you and Gerick that I should know about?"

Ayn wanted to tell him the whole story, but that would leave her weak and vulnerable and she couldn't put herself in such a position. Not now, not with Gerick only a few minutes away. She took a deep breath. "You'll have to ask Gerick about that."

"I did," Jonathan said, guiding the car down the ramp.

Ayn's heart skipped several beats as she waited for him to finish.

"Gerick said to ask you."

"I told you, we—"

"I know, I know, the two of you were at Juilliard at the same time. I can tell when I'm being given the runaround, so I'll let it go for now." Jonathan tapped the steering wheel impatiently. "But whatever it is between the two of you, I hope you work it out, and soon. We have a season approaching fast."

Ayn rolled down her window, allowing the warm air of mid-September to sweep through the small sedan. "Don't worry, Jonathan. I am a professional and I have the good of the orchestra first on my mind." To herself she added, and second in my heart. Something had happened to her in the span of twenty-four hours, something she had no resistance to; she was falling in love with him again. She sighed, wondering if she had ever fallen out of love with Gerick.

Ayn glanced out the window to Main Street as they drove past a white clapboard mansion. The house was a classic design in Greek Revival with large, two-story columns across the front.

"Usually you're chatting about how peaceful and relaxing it is here when we pass the Hadwen House," Jonathan said.

"There are still too many tourists this time of year," she answered, leaning against the headrest and closing her eyes.

"There it is," Jonathan said, interrupting her thoughts. "My home away from home."

Ayn opened her eyes and stared across the sand. The afternoon sun was high and reflected gold off the cedar shingles of the lean-to style house. Jonathan parked his car by the side of the beach house. As Ayn stepped from the sedan she heard the first phrase of the Tchaikovsky Concerto coming from inside. She froze, transfixed by the beauty of Gerick's pure tone. Ayn gasped at his ability to make the violin sing with such a silvery ring while at the same time making it sound so big, so full of expression.

Jonathan struggled past her with several pieces of luggage. "Can you deny that this is the most extraordinary voice ever played?"

Ayn gave a small smile. "No," she said, taking a couple of flight bags to relieve his burden. "I can't deny he's the best."

As they rounded the corner of the house, Gerick's sweet, velvety chords became louder. Ayn paused when she reached the top step of the deck. Gerick was just inside the open patio doors. She couldn't take her eyes off him and wondered if she would experience the same thrilling but terrifying sensations every time she saw him.

His tall, muscled body was profiled to her and she felt an empty ache ignite and spread through her. Dressed in tight-fitting jeans and knit polo shirt, Gerick was totally absorbed in his music. His body glided in powerful movements as he poured himself into the small instrument resting beneath his chin. The lines of his face seemed to be expressing exquisite joy and pain simultaneously. She knew that this was the moment the composer had dreamed his notes would inspire. For an instant she felt joined with him in a world where the only emotions that existed were those created by the music.

Ayn pulled herself from the daze when she sensed Jonathan behind her. Turning, she noticed Jonathan's green eyes were wet with tears. He made no effort to hide the feelings that Gerick's playing stirred in him. "You're an old softy," Ayn said softly, then leaned down and kissed him on the cheek.

Almost at the same moment Gerick's violin went flat. The sour note was hardly heard before his oath pierced the gentle sea air. Jonathan rushed past Ayn and was halfway across the deck when Gerick's indignant strides brought him to meet the older man.

Gerick could barely restrain his smoldering temper. Holding the tiny neck of his instrument, he shook it violently. "Did you hear that?" he said. "A Guarneri! And it went flat. It's this damn sea air! Why in the name of all that is sacred would you purchase a house surrounded by such dampness?"

Gerick paced the redwood floor in front of Jonathan, who was trying to appear as concerned as his guest. Gerick sliced the air with his bow. "A conductor, of all people, should know that this salt air is treacherous to musical instruments."

Jonathan calmly set the bags down and took the violin and bow from Gerick. Ayn wore her "I told you so" smile when she walked between the two men. "A temperamental superstar," she repeated to Jonathan.

Gerick whirled on his heel to face her. "A little professional jealousy?"

Ayn turned to face him. "Why don't you quit

blaming Jonathan's house for your own faults?" Ayn asked, her words as harsh as the look she now wore on her face.

"Why don't you mind your own business, Ms. Remington?"

"Don't yell at me because you can't handle a piece as simple as the Concerto," she snapped, setting the luggage on the deck with a thud.

Gerick matched her stance, his feet apart, fists balled and resting on his hips. "I'll yell at anyone I please, and right now it pleases me to yell at a little prima donna who is running from her own talent."

Ayn moved toward him and tried not to show her surprise when he matched her steps. She told herself it was anger drawing them together, but the passion surfacing in his blue eyes belied her excuse. She refused to back down. "If we're going to get into careers, lets start with yours. *I* made you what you are today."

"*You* made me?" He threw his head back and let the ominous laugh explode. "Ha!"

They were inches apart, their bodies trembling with the heat of the argument.

"If I hadn't walked out on you—"

"If *you* hadn't walked out on *me!* I made you leave. Just like now, you don't have the courage to—"

"You want courage," she shouted. "I'll show you courage." She drew her hand back, but Gerick's strong fingers curled around her wrist before she could make contact with her target. He pulled her to him and held her so tightly she could hardly catch her breath.

From behind her came Jonathan's weak voice. "I think I hear a can of tuna fish calling me. Excuse me while I check on lunch."

Jonathan's timid footsteps crossed the deck and faded into the carpeting. When she was sure he was out of earshot, she took a deep breath and prepared for word battle with Gerick. She looked up at him and saw that he had softened. His clear blue eyes no longer burned with hatred; instead she saw the same sad, knowing look she'd seen ten years ago. Slowly he released his grip on her wrist.

"Gerick, I . . ."

"Sh-h-h," he breathed softly.

He had released her, but she still felt the embrace of his gaze. She searched his eyes for a hint to his true feelings; all she found was pain. They moved apart at the same time, and, feeling slightly dazed, she walked to where she'd dropped the bags.

"Allow me," he said, quietly moving to stand beside her. Ayn nodded and started to look at him; then she stopped. He was right, she was running, but not from her talent. She was a coward only when it came to facing Gerick and her love for him. One look, one touch at a moment like this and she would bind her heart to him forever. She lowered her gaze and preceded him into the house.

"Well," Jonathan said as they entered the combination living and dining room. "Now that the yelling is over, we have a lot of work to do." He carried a large plate of fresh fruit from the kitchenette and placed it on a circular table. "But first, we eat."

"Let me help you," Ayn offered, coming back to life.

"It's ready," Jonathan said, grinning.

"I'd like to apologize," Gerick started.

"No need for that," Jonathan said, and laughed. "You're right, this is not an ideal home for a musician, but when I'm here it's usually to get away from music. Of course, there are times when Ayn talks me into a quiet working weekend here." He picked a grape from the plate and popped it into his mouth. "But I play the piano so poorly that we can't tell if it's in tune or not."

Ayn was careful to make sure Jonathan was between her and Gerick when they sat at the table. She was thankful that Jonathan kept the conversation light during the meal and that he deliberately avoided any reference to the scene on the patio. Before long, Jonathan had led them into a discussion of music and the food was pushed aside so folds of sheet music could be spread in every available space.

The tension that first existed eased quickly into a comfortable working arrangement. Although Ayn was constantly aware of her natural reaction to Gerick, she was happy to find she could put her feelings aside and work closely with him. Notes ran into phrases and phrases into entire movements as the hours passed.

It wasn't until the shrill ring of the telephone startled her that Ayn realized she was actually sitting beside Gerick playing a duet with him. Her fingers faltered and she wanted to pull away, but his concentration never waned. She took a deep breath and tried to focus her attention on the keys in front of her. Again the phone rang.

Jonathan was leaning on the back of the piano and

he slammed his palm down on the wood. "I should have had that thing disconnected," he mumbled, walking past them toward the kitchen area.

Immediately the space around Ayn and Gerick seemed to grow smaller. She realized when he left that it had been Jonathan who had drawn them into a world totally of music. It was his presence that had kept them both on a professional level. Jonathan was truly a master conductor. She stopped playing, thinking she would never be able to gain such control as a conductor.

"No, no," Jonathan called as he picked up the receiver, "keep playing."

Ayn shook her head. She rose quickly and moved away from the piano. "Stay," Gerick said, his low voice blending with the Brahms melody.

She stopped, seeing nothing through the mist in her eyes. Why hadn't he asked her to stay ten years ago? Slowly she blinked the tears away. She answered softly. "I want to clean up this mess."

Still refusing to face him, Ayn busied herself picking up the dishes they'd left from lunch. She walked into the kitchenette and began running hot water over the plates. Gerick was still playing, and she increased the water pressure hoping to drown him out. Then she noticed Jonathan was leaning against the wall, the receiver held to one ear and his hand covering his other ear.

"Sorry," she said, and turned off the faucet. As she grabbed a towel to dry her hands, she realized the house was silent. Then he began the soft, low rhapsody that Ayn loved. Every time she heard the whispered promise in the strong, masculine notes of the opening bars, she thought of Gerick, and now he was playing it for her. The passage was a brilliant blend of pain and loneliness mysteriously combined with erupting joy.

Before she realized that she had moved, Ayn was standing behind Gerick. Her hands were on his shoulders and she was watching his fluid motion as he lightly touched the keys. He laid his cheek on her hand, then kissed her fingertips. The thrill that coursed through her veins was no longer created by the rising emotions of the opus.

Ayn sat next to Gerick as he began the crescendo just before the coda. He built to such a climax that she resented the noble way he brought the piece back to its original haunting phrase. Closing on a note that spoke of a love that had been and had died, he turned to face her.

Ayn was transfixed by his stare. That intense, demanding stare which always left her breathless. The moment hung between them, charged with unfulfilled passion. His eyes shimmered with desire as he read her face and she realized she had never stopped wanting and needing him.

She knew her voice would sound weak, but she forced the words from her throat. "And the critics say you're afraid of the romantic composers like Rachmaninoff."

"I am," he said, his voice a low timbre. "I hide behind a classic repertoire. Beethoven's Violin Concerto is hardly more than scales and arpeggios. When there is very little melody, there is very little chance of letting your emotions show as is necessary with A Theme of Paganini."

"But just now, I saw you . . ."

Ayn forgot how strong a violinist's hands were

until his fingers were biting into the soft flesh of her upper arms. He pulled her closer to him. "Yes, *you* saw it. On stage I bare my soul to the world, but there is a part of me I can reveal to no one. No one but you, Ayn."

Her hands were trembling as she reached up and stroked his cheek. Suddenly the lines of his face hardened and he broke the spell his gaze held her in. Ayn didn't try to mask the confusion she felt as she studied his harsh features. Then she heard Jonathan clear his throat.

Gerick lifted his gaze briefly from Ayn to Jonathan. "We were just discussing Rachmaninoff."

"Yes," Jonathan said with a laugh. "Rachmaninoff affects me the same way. Say, while we're on the subject of Russian composers, that call was very interesting."

Ayn turned to face Jonathan, and hoped that Gerick would release his hold on her.

He did release her momentarily, but then he draped his arm around her shoulder. Her irritation at Gerick's obvious display of possessiveness was replaced with concern when she looked at the conductor's face.

"Jonathan!" She stood instantly and rushed to the older man. "Are you all right? You look so pale."

Jonathan shook his head and motioned her away from him. "I'm fine, just a little tired, that's all." He moved further into the room and sat on the sofa. "You two just tried to work an old man to death, that's all. Do you realize we've been at this for over five hours without a break?"

Gerick rose and moved to sit beside Jonathan.

Ayn knew Gerick had noticed a change in his friend too, but Gerick was careful not to let it show as she had. "So, what was the call about?"

Jonathan smiled. "Things are looking good for the cultural exchange with Russia. It appears our symphony may be spending Christmas in Moscow."

Ayn clapped her hands together and plopped down beside Jonathan. "Oh, wouldn't that be grand. Imagine St. Basil's Cathedral on a snowy night in Red Square."

"Ayn's our resident romantic," Jonathan said, and his laugh filled the room. Ayn sneered at him, but was glad to see his coloring had returned to normal. "Anyway," the conductor continued, "I need to drive back to the city. There are still some details to be worked out."

"Tonight?" Ayn questioned, glancing through the glass door to the failing light of the late afternoon. "It'll be dark before you reach New York."

Jonathan patted her arm and looked at Gerick. "There are a few disadvantages to having a woman as your assistant conductor." He turned back to Ayn. "I promise to drive under the speed limit all the way and have the car home by midnight."

Gerick fell against the back of the sofa with a burst of laughter.

"Don't encourage him," Ayn said. Then she turned back to Jonathan. "Well, it's lucky we haven't unpacked yet."

"No, it's a lucky thing *I* haven't unpacked yet. You're staying here and working."

She noticed Gerick rubbing his lips trying to hide his smile. Suddenly the full realization hit her. If she didn't go back with Jonathan, she and Gerick would be alone there for two whole days. The thought was enticing but dangerous. "No, I came with you, and I'm going home with you. It's a long drive to make by yourself, especially after a day like we've had. Besides, you still look—"

Jonathan's eyes snapped with anger. "I am perfectly fit and more than capable of driving back to the city *alone*." He stood and walked toward his bedroom.

"But—"

"Need I remind you I am the conductor and you are the assistant? You do as I say, and I say there is too much work here that is unfinished."

He disappeared down the hallway as Ayn folded her arms across her chest. "Stubborn old fool," she said, allowing her mouth to fall into a pout.

"I heard that," Jonathan called from his bedroom.

"I meant for you to," she yelled back. He reappeared with his luggage and Gerick jumped to his feet. He took Jonathan's bags. "I'll load the car for you."

Jonathan nodded, but didn't follow Gerick outside; instead he stared at Ayn. She glanced up at him and he opened his arms to her. She smiled at his invitation and stood to accept his bear hug. Together they walked outside to join Gerick.

"You don't mind bringing Ayn back to New York, do you?" Jonathan asked, shaking Gerick's hand.

"I don't mind at all," Gerick said, a curious look passing between the two men.

Ayn started to talk, but Jonathan cut her off. "Now, I expect you to come back with two seasons firmed up, one for Russia and one for another Back Roads America tour, just in case something goes wrong." He seated himself inside the car. "You're going to be very busy, so if I may suggest, not too many discussions on Rachmaninoff." Then, with a quick salute, Jonathan sped away.

Ayn shoved her hands into the side pockets of her wide circle skirt. Now that they were alone, she became aware that the one-shoulder blouse with a diagonal ruffle across her breast was probably not a good choice for the occasion. She rocked on her heels as she watched Jonathan's car become a small dot in the distance, and tried to think of what to do next.

"Come on," Gerick said, nudging her shoulder as though they were old buddies. "Let's take a walk on the beach before we get back to work."

Gerick slipped off his boat-styled oxfords and tossed them onto the deck before Ayn had untied the ankle strap on one of her sandals. "At this rate it will be a moonlight walk. Here, let me help."

He bent and lifted her foot to rest on his knee as Ayn's protest died in her throat. His long fingers loosened the bow and began to unlace the strap around her ankle quickly; then his hands slowed and finally they stopped. How could something so seemingly innocent feel so intimate? Gerick had felt it too. That was the reason he had stopped and was now staring at her. Without taking his eyes off of her, Gerick placed his hand on her calf and lifted her leg slightly as he removed the sandal with his other hand.

Ayn forced herself to swallow and tried to clear

her mind of the nagging questions which threatened to spoil the moment. Questions about their past, their present and their future. She closed her eyes and shook her head slightly. No, she couldn't let it happen. There were too many questions that had the wrong answer, or worse, no answer at all.

When she opened her eyes Gerick was rising slowly. He was so near that she ached to rediscover the feel of his flesh with her exploring fingers. Not daring to meet his eyes again, Ayn locked her gaze on the tiny animal stitched on his polo shirt directly in front of her. She knew she could get lost in that liquid blue stare of his, lost forever.

"Ayn," he whispered. "Look at me."

Her voice was faint at first but she managed to answer him. "I thought we were going for a walk." With a determination she wasn't sure she possessed, Ayn willed her legs to move and started away.

Gerick's hand reached out to a redwood beam supporting the deck and his arm blocked her retreat. Ayn sighed; she knew she didn't have the emotional strength to fight him. She turned to move in the opposite direction, but he closed the trap with a quick movement of his right arm. Ayn tried to put space between them, but her back met the wooden post. Gerick closed the small distance between their bodies until the solid wall of his chest was forcing the evidence of his labored breathing against the rise and fall of her own breast.

Ayn's body trembled and she felt helpless against her senses. Her fear of what might happen was only equaled by her fear of what might not happen. She felt hollow, and yet there was a warmth glowing and growing inside her. Gerick placed the tip of his finger under her chin, but Ayn refused to look up; instead she turned her head away and glanced down.

"Look at me," he said, his voice a low growl.

Reluctantly she allowed him to tilt her head back until their eyes met. Without a word, they seemed to speak of all their yesterdays as they continued to stare at each other. Memories of the gentle times they'd shared played through her mind, and she smiled. Gerick's features mirrored the same happiness and she knew he was remembering how it had once been for them. For an instant, looking into his laughing eyes she experienced a glimmer of hope that they might recapture those times again. Then another picture played before her mind and she sobered.

A coldness swept through her, like the wind on that winter morning when a part of her had died. Gerick stiffened and his eyes became hard like brilliant blue stones. Suddenly, his palm pounded the redwood beam and a curse split the calm air as he turned away from her.

"I can't stand that hurt look in your eyes."

For the first time Ayn truly believed that he had suffered as she had; she realized he'd felt the loneliness too. What fools they were. She placed her hand on his arm as a tenderness enveloped her. "Why did we stay apart for so long?"

Gerick shook free of her touch, then turned to face her. His eyes blazed with anger. "What was I supposed to do, crawl?"

"No," she answered, surprised. "I—"

"A man can only bend so much, Ayn. Why didn't *you* come back to me?"

He'd struck a nerve. "I see," she said softly, her

words dripping with venom. "A man can't crawl, but a woman can, right?"

He sighed with disgust. "I'm trying to talk about us, and you're making a feminist issue out of it."

"You're right, Gerick, it's not a feminist issue. It's a dead issue, and as far as I'm concerned, it should remain that way. Dead!" She pivoted and let her anger carry her across the grassy dunes to the beach.

The late-afternoon breeze carried the tangy sea air to her long before she crested the dunes and ran onto the wet gray sand. She inhaled several deep breaths hoping to clear her thoughts. Why had she snapped at him? Was anger the only defense against their passion?

Deep in a cross-examination of her emotional scars, Ayn gave a start when Gerick fell into stride beside her. Hands clasped together behind his back, he didn't say a word, but seemed to be inching closer to her as they walked. Ayn moved over until she was ankle deep in the surf.

"I suppose it's useless to have this conversation now, but I want you to know that you're the main reason I decided to do an entire season with Interurban Symphony Orchestra." He paused, but Ayn offered no comment. "Not you, the woman I loved; but you, the associate conductor."

Still not speaking, Ayn lifted her skirt slightly and moved further into the water to keep a safe distance between them. Gerick moved in front of her and it took every ounce of willpower for Ayn not to step back. She tipped her head and gave him a defiant look.

"Thank you," she snapped, and walked around

him. Gerick's hand clamped on her arm and he whirled her around. The hem of her skirt skimmed the surface and sent a spray of water in every direction as she spun around to face him.

"You don't believe me, do you?"

"No," she answered, matching his angry glare.

"Well, you should. ISO is probably the youngest orchestra in the nation, and yet look at the recognition it is receiving, not to mention the financial support. People are begging to give you grants."

Ayn smiled. "I'll admit, a few years ago it seemed an impossible task to get and keep this company on its feet."

"The difference has been you, Ayn. Ever since you and Jonathan joined forces, ISO has become what it was intended to be, an orchestra for the American people. Your concept of taking symphony music down the back roads to the small towns and communities that haven't had any exposure to a philharmonic gave ISO the direction it needed."

He paused, but Ayn refused to look at him. She didn't want him to look in her eyes and see how desperately she wanted to believe that he meant what he was saying.

If he was upset by her apparent lack of interest, he didn't show it when he continued in the same tone. "Now, the big cities are standing in line to get you to come to them. Why, even Russia wants to take a closer look at you. They want to see just what it is that makes the orchestra so special. And the answer is standing right in front of me."

"Would you like to hire on as my agent?" she laughed.

"I guess I did get a bit carried away."

Ayn nodded. "You seem to know more about me than I do."

"You've done a great job, even if you are a woman."

Ayn's eyes narrowed, but the smile on Gerick's face dispelled her worries. "I'm just kidding. I'm not an ogre." He stepped closer to her. "I'm proud to say you're the woman I've loved since the first day I saw you."

Panic tore through her. "No! Gerick, don't say things like that. I won't let us confuse our passion for each other with love, not this time."

He pulled her closer to him and his strong arms circled her waist, holding her captive. "Call it what you will, Ayn, but I want you. I always have."

The hunger in his blue eyes sent a shiver of desire quaking through her as he pulled her closer. Ayn braced her hands against his chest, feeling the muscled strength beneath her fingers. Slowly, his mouth drifted to the parted softness of her lips. Gentle, almost teasing at first touch, he gathered her tight within his hold and his kiss unleashed the need that had been raging inside them for years.

Ayn clung to him and arched her back against the sensations that snaked through her. He seemed to be devouring her soul with the breathless passion of his kiss, and her head began to swim with dizziness as he drained all resistance from her. When he began to trace a trail of velvet kisses down her cheek, Ayn moaned with a pleasure she had forgotten existed.

His erotic journey ended at the hollow behind her ear. The sound of his ragged breath so near caused a trembling ache within her. Gerick groaned and began to place feather-soft kisses along her sensitive neck. She gasped and his mouth quickly smothered her plea.

Suddenly Ayn became aware that the lapping waves around their legs had grown choppy. Gerick pulled away and they both turned to look out to sea. Dark rolling clouds seemed to be chewing up the bright orange ball of the setting sun and the waves were whitecapped.

Gerick took her by the arm. "We'd better get inside before a storm breaks loose."

Ayn nodded. She didn't want the kiss to end, but she told herself she had to accept it for what it was, a fleeting moment when their emotions overrode their minds. She started inland. Gerick allowed her arm to slip through his hand, but he tightened his hold when her wrist was about to escape him.

She hesitated, then looked back at Gerick.

"You do realize what's going to happen if we stay here together?" Gerick asked, his blue eyes challenging her brown ones.

She felt her heart grow heavy as the reality of the situation forced itself upon her. She looked at Gerick and realized her moment of contemplation had allowed a glimmer of hope to show on his face. Ayn shook her head. "We'd better go back to the city," she answered softly.

"Yes," he said, dropping her hand.

Ayn watched the proud carriage of his tall frame as Gerick walked past her. She wondered if she had made the right choice, and began to follow his path across the dunes. No matter what she labeled her feelings for Gerick, need, desire or love, she wanted him with a conviction that scared her. Still, if she gave in, would she have the courage to face the consequences?

Forcing the thoughts from her mind, she climbed the stairs and crossed the deck. Gerick had remained at least ten steps in front of her, never glancing back. Now as she entered the house, she heard a door down the hall being slammed closed. She felt a strange sense of rejection. It wasn't just that he had shut her out of the room, but he had shut her out of his life again.

The sound of running water came from Gerick's bath and she walked down the hall toward her own room. It was better this way. They needed to go back to the city, back where there were people and things to keep both of them thinking clearly.

"Ayn?" Gerick called. "There aren't any towels in here. Would you bring me one?"

She cursed Jonathan for keeping the linens in the hall closet as she grabbed a towel and started for Gerick's room. Crossing his bedroom, she saw the door to the bath was ajar.

"Damn you, Gerick Grier," she swore.

She considered dropping the towel just inside the door and running, but she didn't want to give him the pleasure of seeing her squirm. Ayn pushed the door open and stepped inside, keeping her back to the shower. "Your towel is on the vanity," she called.

Gerick didn't answer, but a curl of steam rushed out as the shower door slid open. Ayn glanced up into the mirror and saw Gerick standing in the middle of a wet cloud behind her. She turned around to face him and leaned against the vanity for support. Her eyes were riveted to the muscled lines of his tanned body. He'd taken on the sinewy form of a grown man since the last time she'd seen him without his clothes.

Slowly he reached out to her. She slipped her hand into the warmth of his. "Forget New York," he said, pulling her into the steamy shower.

"This is—" she started, but Gerick kissed her.

Ayn laced his black-and-silver hair through her fingers and pulled him closer to her. His dripping body soaked her clothes instantly, but she ignored the wetness all around her. With deliberate joy she began to explore the curve of his bottom lip with her tongue. Gerick answered her with a probing exploration of his own.

The damp cotton material clung to her like a second skin, but she ached to feel the smooth texture of flesh on flesh. As if he'd read her thoughts, Gerick freed the hem of her blouse from the waistband and eased it over her head. With a flick of his wrist he gently tossed the ruffled blouse over the top of the stall. Then he feathered a trail of kisses from the creamy softness of her shoulder to the taut peaks of her swelling breast.

His kisses were like liquid fire as he expertly drew a shuddered response from her. She took in a sharp breath as his hands slid beneath the gathered waistband of her skirt. With one swift motion, her skirt and panties lay in a wet heap at her feet. Gerick leaned down to help her step from the circle of material and the full force of the shower pelted her body. Ayn reveled in the pulsating heat and leaned against the tiled wall of the shower; then Gerick rose to tower above her again.

He smiled appreciatively as his gaze fixed on her nude body. Ayn felt her legs grow weak and she wasn't sure if she could support her own weight. Hesitantly she reached out and let her fingers trace the dark, swirling hair on Gerick's chest. He touched her hands, then held them in one of his. With his other hand Gerick poured a generous portion of liquid soap over their hands. His blue eyes sparkled as he stared at her while they worked the creamy soap into a bubbling lather.

Gerick's large hands began to smooth the suds up her arms. Ayn followed his lead, enjoying the sensation of his coarse hair mixing with the soothing lubricant. The fragrance of cucumber and elder flower filled the steamy bath. The scent was fresh and exhilarating as they rediscovered the beauty and secrets of each other.

Gerick's hands slipped down her sides to the small roundness of her hips and he pulled her to him. Ayn locked her hands behind his neck and molded her frame to the rangy contours of his. Again his mouth covered hers, demanding a completeness that sent a shiver down her spine. She was conscious of the hard male outline that burned against her thighs, and she longed to have him fill the emptiness inside her.

Suddenly he waltzed her under the shower spray and she felt the delicate lather wash from their bodies. Gerick broke the kiss and reached out to turn off the water. Ayn looked up at him in surprise.

"I want to enjoy every minute of this," he said, pulling her to him roughly. He opened the door, and after quickly toweling them off, he lifted her from the ground and gathered her into his powerful arms. Ayn relaxed against him as they stepped from the bath into the bedroom.

Gerick carried her to the bed and laid her on the velvety softness of the spread. For a moment she wanted to protest, but one look at his eyes sent all rational thoughts from her mind. The mattress sagged under his weight and she became aware only of his hard, lean body next to hers. Gerick bent over her, drawing tiny circles of moisture with his tongue on the flat plane of her stomach. Ayn trembled anxiously as his roaming hands began to massage her thighs. His deliberate caress sent a languorous feeling on a leisurely pace through her lower limbs. Gerick's teasing hand only added kindling to the burning flame that was already raging within her dark, throbbing recesses.

"Oh, Gerick," she whispered.

He moaned and rolled on top of her. She felt the promise of his love straining between the parted softness of her legs and arched her back to accept him. A small cry tore from her throat as he entered her, creating an exquisite blend of pain and joy.

Like the magnitude of a thousand-piece orchestra in perfect synchronization, she couldn't comprehend the overwhelming pleasure that surrounded her. Joy seemed to be bursting inside her, begging to be released. Gerick was drawing everything from her yet giving back more than he took. Ayn felt as though she were venturing into his soul, and she wanted desperately to learn the mysteries hidden there.

From a height she'd never known, Gerick plunged her down, down as though she were a living flow of music. Then he quickly brought her up again, higher, still higher than before. A dam of emotions exploded within her and Gerick was swept into the swirling pleasure.

Chapter Five

*A*yn felt good, really good, from the inside out, but she wasn't ready to pull herself completely awake. Instead, she rolled over and snuggled into the comforting softness of the bedcovers. The noise of water hitting the porcelain tub mingled with the constant sound of the waves breaking on the nearby shore. Ayn smiled picturing Gerick's lean, muscular body beneath the spray of the shower. She could almost see the water bead in the dark mat of hair on his chest. In her mind's eye, she followed the drop-lets' path as they trickled down the plane of his tautly drawn stomach.

To suppress the giggle that was born of her delicious thoughts, Ayn bit her top lip. She stretched, bringing her senses to full awareness. Then, as she relaxed against the cool crispness of morning sheets, the shower stopped. Looking around, Ayn smiled again. Everything was particularly brilliant, from the hunter's green of the room to the salty smell of the sea breeze which billowed the organdy curtains. But the most brilliant of all was her body's keen memory of the previous night of love.

The bathroom door opened and Ayn quickly closed her eyes. She questioned the silliness of her gesture and realized she had experienced a sudden moment of doubt. At the instant of facing him, a question had raced through her mind. What if he wasn't as happy as she was about their reunion? The thought that the wonder of the previous night might have been nothing more than a moment of passion to him was something she wasn't ready to accept.

Pretending to still be asleep, Ayn managed to watch him through a tiny slit between her lids. Standing with his back to her at the triple dresser, he began to brush his damp hair away from his forehead. The streak of silver glistened like a diamond on black velvet. Suddenly he stopped in midstroke and stared into the mirror. His gaze was riveted on Ayn, and the look on his face relieved all of her fears. It was a look of tenderness, of need, and of a hurt which kept that need in check. Placing his palms on the dresser, he leaned forward and dropped his head.

Quietly, Ayn rose from the bed and went to him. She slipped her arms around his chest and hugged him close. Before she could rest her head against his back, he turned, the circle of his arms surrounding her. His embrace was desperate, as though he would never let her go, and she understood that it was the hug he'd wanted to give ten years earlier.

"Do you know the number of times I've remembered how helpless you look in your sleep and let the memory tear me apart inside? I've imagined the mahogany fan of your hair on the pillow next to mine so many times, a minute ago I thought it was all a dream again."

The battle against her tears was lost and she barely choked out her words. "We're a couple of fools."

Placing his fingers beneath her chin, he tilted her head back. "No more hurting, Ayn, I swear, there'll be no more hurting."

Her smile was full and uninhibited, until she caught herself and drew her lips together. Gerick traced the tiny dimple on her cheek with the backs of his fingers. "The smile I love the best." The look that passed between them spoke more than any words could have, and Ayn watched as his lips curved into a sensuous smile. His head dipped and she stood on her toes to meet him. Their kiss was deliberate and sweet, like the first taste of freedom savored by a prisoner.

Gerick pulled away and placed his finger on Ayn's mouth to quiet her protest. "Hurry and get dressed. I have a surprise for you."

She laced her fingers around his neck. "Better than this?" Again she reached to meet a kiss.

Gerick laughed. "Well, no, but almost." He gently unwound her hands and turned her toward the bathroom. "I'll put the coffee on."

Reluctantly Ayn gathered her kimono and started toward the shower while Gerick gave one last check in the mirror. She stopped and turned to face him. "What's the surprise?"

"If I told you, then it wouldn't be a surprise,

would it?" He shooed her on with a wave of his hand. "I worked on it all yesterday morning while I was waiting for you and Jonathan. Now hurry!"

Ayn showered quickly and dressed in jeans and a lilac-colored tee shirt with a scoop neck and shirred shoulders that ended in a tight cuff at the elbow. She could hardly keep from smiling as she applied lip gloss and mascara. Then, she became so impatient with brushing her hair that she stopped short of her usual routine. Shrugging at her disheveled image in the mirror, she tossed the brush on the bed and rushed out of the bedroom.

The desire to see Gerick immediately caused her to literally bounce down the hallway, but she paused at the entrance to the living area. Lounging against the doorframe, she studied him as he sorted through a stack of the scores. She admired the way the Jacquard sweater clung snugly to his broad chest. It was white with three large stripes in shades varying from gray to black, and it blended well with the black and silver of his hair. Still deep in his search, he bent down and his muscled thighs expanded the black denim of his form-fitting jeans.

"Ah-ha!" he said, pulling the composition from its hiding place. Turning, he grinned when he saw Ayn watching him.

She folded her arms. "I'm waiting for my surprise."

"Coming right up," he answered, arranging the sheets on the stand. With a dramatic flare he picked up his Guarneri and posed the bow above the strings.

Ayn knew every piece they'd brought and she wondered what he would think was so special. As he began to play, she felt as though she'd been slapped. It was the overture of her own symphony. She straightened, but refrained from telling him to stop. He glanced at her and she forced a smile. The look on his face was like that of a small boy wanting desperately to please his new friend, and she couldn't let him know how upset she was. She herself was surprised by the amount of anger within her. If it had been anyone else playing her music she would have been irritated, but only Gerick could make her feel so hostile. She knew then that his opinion of her meant more than anyone else's, even Jonathan's.

Again, Gerick glanced at her. His fingers tripped over the notes and he paused.

"Don't stop," she said, and swallowed back her own feelings. "Please, go on."

"You're not happy, are you?"

She sighed. It was no use trying to hide her thoughts from Gerick; he knew her too well. "No, but I know I should be. I should be flattered. I should . . ." She couldn't go on. A strange hurt brought tears to her eyes.

"Ayn, I only wanted to . . ."

She didn't hear the rest of his explanation because she was hurrying out the sliding glass door. The room had seemed to be suffocating Ayn with her own thoughts, and she had felt the need to flee. But the air on the deck was even more humid than it had been inside. The threatening storm from the evening before had never kept its promise, but neither had it relinquished its hold on the island, and a dense fog hung around her.

The fog masked his approach, and Ayn almost

jumped when Gerick was suddenly beside her. The inviting smell of freshly brewed coffee wafted to her. He handed her a mug, then leaned against the rail and stared out to where the shore should be.

"I'm sorry," she said, also staring straight ahead. "But it made me angry for you to play my overture before it's ready." She took a quick sip of her coffee before she added, "More than that, it made me feel as though you'd invaded my most private thoughts."

"Believe me, Ayn, I wouldn't have attempted to play the symphony if I'd known. I thought it was finished, ready to be given life."

She looked at him carefully, wondering if he meant it. "If you thought it was so ready, why did you change the pizzicato?"

"You know the answer to that better than I do. It's what sets us apart from third- or fourth-chair musicians. In every piece we pick up we see a chance to try something a little different to see if our interpretation is what the composer might have been thinking of when he created it. I've heard you say yourself, sometimes even Beethoven wasn't entirely aware of what he was trying to bring together." He drained the last of his coffee and set the mug on the railing. "Didn't you think it sounded better when I used the tip of my finger instead of the flesh part?"

"Of course it sounded better. Why else would it have upset me so?" She offered him a half smile. "And why is it I can never stay mad at you?"

Expecting a flippant answer about his good looks or charm, she was surprised when he spoke seriously.

"Because the same thing that tears us apart,

inevitably pulls us together again: music. We perceive it the same way. Do you know how long it's been since I've had a stimulating conversation about music? No one understands or has the same passions I do except you. We're good for each other."

She set her mug beside his and shoved her hands into the pockets of her jeans. "Good for each other, I'm not sure—but we do need each other."

Gerick slipped his arm through hers and urged her toward the steps. "Let's walk."

She agreed even though they couldn't see more than a few yards in front of them. Following the muted sound of the waves lapping against the sand, they found the beach. "I've spent years touring the country, end to end," Ayn said. "And each step, each day should have taken me further away from you. I realized today that it didn't. I've been harboring a hope that I'd find you waiting for me around every curve in the road."

"My hope was that I'd turn and see you running after me."

"What happened to us?" Ayn asked.

"I guess we thought we had to sacrifice our love for our careers."

"How noble we are when we're young." They fell silent until Ayn stopped and Gerick turned to face her. "Why did you feel you had to compete with me?"

He carefully brushed a damp lock of hair from her temple. "For the same reason you feel you must compete with me."

"But I don't feel that way."

His look was knowing. "You will. We've gone our

separate ways, both striving to capture the top. Now we'll be working together, and now our struggle will become more intense."

She looked away from the mesmerizing blue of his eyes to keep her thoughts clear. "But you've reached the top. You can relax."

He laughed. "I don't believe for a moment that you really think that. You've made it far enough to know it only gets harder, never easier. Once you're officially there you have to stay on that great summit, fighting off every new artist who has his sights set on your position." He draped his arm over her shoulder and they moved again. "The greatest competition is with yourself," he said, pulling her closer. "You must be as good as you can be. As you grow, you learn with each performance that the next one could and should be better." He paused, but she made no comment. "You already feel it, don't you?"

Ayn nodded. "I've understood it from the first day I left Juilliard for the real world, but I've never admitted it before."

In the quiet moment of love that followed, they shared emotions as if they were one person; they needed nothing more than to know they were together. The fog continued to surround them as though creating a world forgotten by men and deity alike.

A gull flew into the realm of their vision with a sudden flurry of sound. Ayn and Gerick stopped, watching the worried circles made by the bird. Then came the cry of its mate, lost in the fog. The gull dipped, arched backward and flew blindly into the haze. They stared after him, each wondering if they would ever have that kind of unquestioning faith in their love.

Ayn took a deep breath before asking the question that had plagued her for ten years. "Those last few weeks, where did you go every night?"

"I had to take a second job."

"Why didn't you tell me? Don't bother, I know the answer already. It was your blasted pride."

Gerick nodded. "I didn't mind. It allowed me to keep some of my self-respect."

"But I would have helped. I could have gotten a job too. We were supposed to share everything, remember?"

"I wanted to tell you. I almost did so many times. Not so you could help out. I'd have worked five different jobs before I'd have let you take one. But so you'd understand and not think I was running around on you, or worse, that I just didn't care anymore."

"So, why didn't you?" Ayn asked, facing him squarely.

"By the time I swallowed enough pride and worked up the nerve, I began to see what was going to happen to us. Then, your job offer came up." He shrugged and gave a sheepish smile. "And the rest is history."

"How did you find out about the San Francisco position? Mr. Edwards swore he'd keep it a secret until I made a decision."

"My night job was janitor at the school. I didn't mean to snoop, but your name was on the piece of paper and I couldn't resist reading it."

Ayn took his hands in hers. "The greatest pair of

hands in the world of music, doing cleanup work. Oh, Gerick, I'm sorry." She kissed the tips of his fingers.

He laughed. "Don't be sorry; it was my decision. Besides, remembering helps to keep me humble." He reversed the position of their hands and cupped hers in his. "Anyway, I'm holding the greatest pair of hands. Mine control one instrument; your hands control a hundred different instruments and make them sound like one."

"If I didn't already love you, I would after hearing you say that."

The dark of his eyes dominated the blue as he stared at her. "Then, you do still love me."

She dropped her gaze for a moment before looking back at him. "I suppose I never stopped loving you."

"Nor I, you."

Suddenly the morning sun began to break through the blue-gray fog. The bright rays of light tried to penetrate the heavy veil and it created a curtain that shimmered like silver glitter. Gerick pointed to a cluster of buildings on the shore. The Old North Wharf had been hidden from their view until the slate blue blanket had rolled its edge back to sea.

"I've heard they call Nantucket 'The Little Gray Lady,'" Ayn said. "Now I know why."

Gerick stared at the distant town as though he were trying to see the weathered details of every shingle. Instinctively Ayn knew she had to be the one who brought it up. Gerick had come back, they'd straightened out the past, and they'd confessed their love. It was her turn to forget pride and to chance getting hurt.

"So, Gerick, what do we do now? Where do we go from here?"

He turned and took her in his arms. The warmth of his embrace made her shiver from the cool dampness around them. "I think we should promise to be honest with each other, even when it might hurt."

"And make a vow against nobility," Ayn added.

"Definitely," he said with a laugh.

"Should we sign in blood?"

Gerick smiled, his eyes growing a deeper shade of blue. Pinpoints of light danced on the silver in his hair as he parted his lips and lowered his head. "I've got a better idea. We'll seal our pledge with a . . ."

His kiss was breathtaking. It seemed to carry her away from the earth to soar among the clouds. She felt as though she were sailing, like the bird who had trusted its flight to the wind, and she prayed she and Gerick would learn to love as completely.

When they reached the beach house the phone was ringing. Annoyed by the intrusion on their world, Ayn didn't attempt to answer.

"It's probably Jonathan," Gerick offered, reaching for the telephone.

"Tell him we've decided to do an entire season of Bach and listen to him yell."

Gerick laughed as he lifted the receiver from its cradle and Ayn checked the coffee to see if it needed warming. The dampness had left her chilled and she rubbed her hands above the heat.

His voice didn't rise in alarm. In fact, what caught Ayn's attention was the drop in his tone. She tensed. Something was terribly wrong. She watched as Gerick scribbled on the pad by the phone, but she didn't look close enough to read it. She didn't want to know yet. Trying not to, she heard Gerick end the call.

". . . yes, yes, we'll be there, right away!" Hanging up, he faced her. "Jonathan's had a heart attack."

Ayn remained calm the entire drive into New York. In fact, she was too calm and it scared Gerick. She'd have to let go soon, and he hoped it would be with him instead of with someone who didn't understand, or worse, when she was alone. He admitted there was a certain amount of selfishness on his part too. She hadn't said she needed him, and Gerick wanted to hear those simple words more than anything else at that moment.

As they became entangled in the midtown traffic, Gerick glanced at her. She sat quietly staring ahead with eyes that were heavy from unshed tears. There was still no sign of release on her face. Gerick wished she'd been able to snuggle beside him so he could hold her close. Somehow he thought the contact would give her strength, but the idea was impossible in the M.G. All he'd been able to do was to hold her hand. Damn the inventor of bucket seats!

Twice during the drive, Ayn had snapped to awareness, her brown eyes wide with fear. Gerick had squeezed her hand in an effort to console her. Then she would offer an automatic smile and slip back into her daze.

The warmth of the Sunday afternoon made the traffic worse than usual. Reluctantly, Gerick released her hand to better maneuver the car. He prayed he hadn't broken her only link with reality.

The parking space was surprisingly close to the hospital and Gerick slipped the car easily into place. He shut off the engine, then turned and draped his arm on the back of her seat. "Are you sure you're up to this?" he asked softly.

Ayn turned to look at him, her features beyond sad. "Yes," was all she said. As their eyes met, Gerick saw a spark beginning to flicker in her glassy stare. For an instant it seemed as though she was going to say something. He held his breath, but when she looked away, the disappointment hurt more than he imagined it could. The frustration made him want to pound his fist against something. Slowly, he reached for the door, only to be stopped by the touch of her hand on his arm. Looking back, he saw a single tear roll down her cheek. "Thank you," she whispered. "I—" She hesitated, then looked away again as if embarrassed.

"Say it, Ayn, go on," he encouraged, silently adding, Say you need me.

"I'm glad you're here," she choked out over the remaining tears. She couldn't say it aloud, but the look in her eyes spoke the words Gerick really wanted to hear. In one swift movement he gathered her close and cradled her against his chest. He'd ached to hear so much more, but what she'd said would have to do—for the moment at least.

He accepted the blame. After all, he'd shoved her out into the world and made her stand on her own. How could he expect her to suddenly let down her defenses and lean on a man who'd let her face so much alone?

Sensing the time was right to move on, they broke the embrace and silently stepped from the car. Ayn waited on the sidewalk as Gerick rounded the front of the car and joined her. Slipping his arm around her, he couldn't help but notice how perfectly she fit by his side.

Just before they reached the glass doors of the hospital, Gerick stopped. "Have you even thought about what's going to happen when we go in there?"

"Yes," she answered too quickly. Then she lowered her gaze. "No. I can't bring myself to think beyond each minute." She looked up, pleading. "I need to see Jonathan. Oh, Gerick, if he dies, I don't know what I'll do. He's my best friend." She paused as if reading his thoughts. "You turned your back on me. Best friends don't do that."

Gerick swallowed hard, collecting his thoughts. "Honesty, even when it hurts, right?"

Ayn nodded as she flattened her palms on his chest and leaned against him. Gerick thought he heard her ask him never to leave her again, but he didn't ask her to repeat it for fear he'd heard wrong. It was easier to accept the statement as what his heart wanted to believe than to chance more pain.

"From what they told me on the phone, Jonathan's condition doesn't sound too serious. There's little danger of losing him."

When she offered no response, Gerick smoothed her hair and became temporarily lost in the softness of the mahogany curls. He thought it strange that his mind should choose that moment to remember exactly how the sun had danced among the strands of her hair on the first day they'd met. He'd always imagined that, with his last breath, that scene would be the final memory of his life. Now, that short time together wasn't enough. Gerick wanted years of loving Ayn and being loved back. He wanted to create so many days together that none could be singled out as more glorious than the others.

He hugged her close and was surprised when he spoke aloud. "We have the lousiest timing." Ayn looked up at him, not trying to hide her confusion. "At the risk of sounding callous, I have to ask if you realize what this is going to mean to your career?"

It only took a second for the shocked look to change to understanding. A mixture of emotions played across her face—hope, sorrow, fear and, finally, confidence. She was ready. Gerick sighed, knowing he'd been right. Again, it was the wrong time for them to try to build a permanent relationship. Jonathan had groomed her well for the conductorship and she was about to become history in the making. A tinge of jealousy tugged at Gerick. He should have been the one who'd helped her grow into the beautiful and complex woman she'd become.

He placed his fingers under her chin and lifted her face until their eyes met. "I'll get you in to see Jonathan. After that you're on your own."

She nodded as they walked on, but Gerick knew she didn't really comprehend what he was talking about.

"Why is it all hospitals look and smell alike?" Ayn asked as they hurried down the gleaming corridor.

"I suppose because they're filled with life and death and the struggle in between."

She shook her head. "You constantly amaze me."

He winked. "Speaking of amazing, here comes Benny Williams, the best public relations director in the city."

Ayn elbowed him. "Hush, he really has done a great job for ISO," she whispered, then said louder, "Benny! Over here."

The wiry man rubbed his hand over his balding head as he rushed toward them. "Thank goodness you're *finally* here."

"We were in Nantucket," Gerick snapped. "We had to wait for the ferry to get off the island."

"Nevertheless, I've had to keep everything on ice until you arrived. Come on."

"Gerick said Jonathan's attack was pretty mild and—"

"Yes," Benny interrupted, motioning for them to hurry.

"What will this mean for—"

"It means ISO could be in big trouble."

Ayn stopped, grabbing Benny's arm. He whirled around to face her, his small eyes full of surprise. "I'm talking about a man's career and possibly his life, and you're—"

Gerick placed a calming hand on her shoulder and continued for her. "What will all of this mean to Jonathan?"

Benny's face was a study in meaningless emotions. "The recovery period will be two or three months, but Jonathan should be able to return to most normal activity soon. Of course, there will be limitations on certain physical endeavors. That will include conducting," he concluded with a shrug.

Ayn slumped against Gerick and his arm went around her for support. With a tenderness Gerick had never seen in the crusty old man, Benny spoke. "Believe me, no one is more upset by this than I am, but we can't afford the luxury of grief now." By the time Benny finished the sentence the coldness had returned to his tone. With Gerick's encouragement Ayn followed the P.R. director. At a turn in the corridor she broke from her numbed silence. "Wait! The sign says the intensive care unit is that way." She pointed in the opposite direction.

"I told you, Ayn, we don't have time for that."

Being a man who'd learned great restraint through the pacing of his music, Gerick spoke in a measured low voice. "I promised Ayn she could see Jonathan before anything else."

"But," Benny started, then stopped when he looked Gerick directly in the eye. "Well, I guess five more minutes won't make that much difference."

"Good!" Gerick said, then turned to Ayn. "Tell the nurse you're family. I'll be waiting here. Benny's going to get the doctor so I can talk with him, aren't you?"

The little man rubbed his head. "Right away," he said, scurrying down the hall.

Gerick patted Ayn's hand, which he held in his, then motioned her on. As he watched her walking away, he could almost see her growing stronger and taller with each step. She was pulling in all her resources. By the time she saw Jonathan, Ayn would have a look of total confidence. Gerick felt a certain regret that she was no longer the woman-child who had trusted his every word to be absolute wisdom. Like the Wizard in the Land of Oz, he felt as though he'd been suddenly stripped of his thunder and lightning. No more was he all-knowing, all-powerful. It had taken him all this time to admit what he'd realized when they'd first met again. She was his equal. The poor little rich girl who'd been pampered and protected by Daddy and then by Gerick was gone.

The same doubt he'd felt earlier returned. The desire that drew them together was stronger than any Gerick had ever seen between two people, but were they right for each other? Could he give her what she needed? He needed her even more than he needed his music. What tore at him was the unanswered question, did she need him?

Ayn could see Jonathan in the glass-walled room. His normally active body was lying very, very still. For the first time since she'd known him, Jonathan looked frail and vulnerable. Tubes and wires from a multitude of machines were attached to him in an orderly confusion. Ayn watched as the miracle of modern medicine attempted to bring life back to the exhausted body of a man who suddenly looked old.

Ayn hesitated inside the doorway. Sensing a presence, Jonathan opened his eyes. His smile was weak, but genuine.

"Well, this is another fine mess we've gotten into," he joked.

Ayn half laughed and half cried as she moved to stand beside him. She took his hand and was relieved by the warmth of his grip. Seeing him close, he looked better than she expected. Gerick was right; it was just a mild attack.

"They'll only let me stay a few minutes, but I had to tell you to concentrate on getting well. Don't worry about a thing. I'll take care of every detail."

"I know you will."

"We'll put all the plans on hold."

"You'll do no such thing."

"Now Jonathan," she said, patting his shoulder.

"Nothing must be stopped or delayed, nothing!" He lifted his hand against her protest. "Don't argue with a sick man."

She smiled. "You've pounded it into my head that we must first and foremost think of the hundred musicians depending on us."

"And the twenty-five-member production crew."

"I know, I know. But surely you don't expect me to—"

"I expect you to do what you were born to do, to become the conductor."

Ayn blinked back the tears. "It's not fair, Jonathan. Why must my big break come from your misfortune?"

"If Bruno Walter had not become ill, would we ever have heard of the young assistant conductor from Boston, a lad named Leonard Bernstein? Or if Sergei Jilinsky had not received the news his poor wife was dying, would I have ever gotten my break in this country? It's the way it works in our world."

A nurse entered the room announcing Ayn's time was up and quickly ushered her out. Ayn saluted him as she walked past the wall of glass, then started up the hall. Gerick was standing at the far end holding several things in his hands and arms. His concerned look caused Ayn to pick up her pace.

"What's wrong?"

"You've got a room full of press people down the hall and they've been waiting quite some time. We'd better hurry."

"A press conference? Here? Now?"

"I tried to warn you, Ayn, but you didn't want to think about it."

"What'll I do? What should I say?" she asked, more to herself than to anyone else. Her mind was clicking with statements and answers to questions even before Gerick replied.

"Let your instincts take over. You'll do fine, but"—he stopped outside a closed door—"you're not going to give the image you should looking like you do."

Ayn glanced down in horror. Her first press conference and she was dressed for the beach.

Gerick offered her the dark blue blazer hanging on his arm. She slipped it on then took the brush from his other hand. "Hope you don't mind. I went through your luggage," he said as he produced a scarf and looped it around her neck. He tied it ascot style to hide the T-shirt she wore. When he buttoned the blazer, his large hands lingered on the last button. She paused and looked up at him. The blue of his eyes was soft yet at the same time intense. The love she saw in his face transported her back in time to the foggy beach where they seemed to be the only two people in the world. There was so much she wanted to tell him, yet she was afraid to admit how deep her feelings were for him. She had trusted him completely once. Like a child, she'd confessed every feeling to him. Feelings that had burst from her with exuberance and joy. She had exposed every inner thought, and then he hadn't wanted her around anymore. He hadn't needed her. A tear trickled down her cheek like the first hesitant drop of rain on a windowpane.

"Oh, Ayn. Please don't cry; not now, darling." He smoothed away the tear with his thumb. "Jonathan will be fine and so will you."

Grateful he didn't understand the real reason for her tears, Ayn fought back the flood that wanted to spill from her. Gerick was right, this wasn't the time or the place to cry.

He reached into the pocket of his jeans and brought out a small bottle. Motioning for her to tilt her head back, he poised the dropper above her eyes. "Blink," he commanded needlessly as the liquid met her eye.

When she'd stopped blinking, Ayn stared up into the vivid blue of Gerick's eyes. The tenderness on his face seemed so out of place with the strength of his features. For half an instant she wanted to forget everything. The conference, the orchestra, even music itself. She wanted to run off to a place where she'd never hear another note. Her heart tore at the absurd thought. There could be no such place for Ayn. Like Beethoven, even if she were totally deaf, she would always hear music playing inside her.

Thick lashes broke the hypnotic spell of his gaze as his eyes looked down to the full curve of her lips. She couldn't help, or even want to change, the eagerness with which she was drawn to him. Again she saw his self-control as he met her with deliberate ease. Ayn tried to restrain the quiver inside her, but his kiss stripped her to the very core of her soul. The crescendo of fluttering excitement left her weak in his arms.

Gently, they parted, but he still looked down at her as though unable to comprehend what he was seeing. Then, like a sudden blast of a foghorn, Benny's voice boomed at her.

"There you are! Hurry, we can't keep them waiting any longer."

Before she could say another word, Ayn was pulled into a small, smoke-filled room. Benny left her at the corner of the podium and stepped up to give the statement on Jonathan's condition. Ayn only half listened as she surveyed the reporters who were jammed into the room. There were four times as many press representatives as she'd ever seen at any function or announcement. A few faces from magazines that had been loyal in their coverage were recognizable, but the majority of people were unknown to Ayn.

". . . And so, to answer your questions as to the future of our company, I now give you the new conductor of the Interurban Symphony Orchestra, Ms. Ayn Remington."

"Ayn Remington, concertmaster" was still repeating in her head as she passed Benny going up to the microphones. He offered her his hand as though in congratulations; then he leaned close and issued a warning. "Be evasive about Gerick. His P.R. man wants him to have his own press conference tomorrow."

Rage temporarily blinded Ayn. Gerick! Of course, that was why so many reporters were here. It wasn't concern over Jonathan, one of the world's greatest conductors, or the fact that Ayn was about to make her debut. It was the rumors they'd heard about the Great Gerick Grier joining with them.

Ayn collected her thoughts quickly and took the podium without the press knowing a part of her had just died. She offered a short statement, then began acknowledging the eager hands of the reporters. It started with the third question.

"Is it true that the Soviet government has approved a tour in their country only now that they suspect Mr. Grier will be a guest soloist with your company?"

"Nothing is settled yet; we're negotiating for a cultural exchange. However, I'm sure you are aware of the enormous amount of red tape involved in any such exchange. This has been in the planning for several months and has nothing to do with recent rumors. The Soviet government has not even decided which of their numerous symphony orchestras they would allow to tour America."

Damn Benny Williams, why didn't he stand up there and tell his own lies? Of course, he referred to them as merely half-truths. She nodded to a reporter from a magazine that had always been supportive of ISO. She hoped his question would relate back to the orchestra. "Ms. Remington, you didn't say if Mr. Grier has joined ISO or not."

"As you're aware, we only have two seasons, winter and summer. The winter season will run December through February, and we are just firming up our plans now." She debated a second, then went ahead with the announcement. "And Mr. Grier will be our guest soloist for that entire season."

At that moment her roving gaze found Gerick, halfway to the back of the room. He was lounging against the wall with his arms folded across his broad chest, but he straightened at her statement. A confused look passed between them and the smile left his face. Ayn stiffened with determination.

The next question came without the reporter

being acknowledged. "Why would a concert violinist of Mr. Grier's stature consider tying himself to one orchestra for several months, especially a relatively new company such as yours?"

Ayn hesitated as she realized that when she forced Gerick to share the limelight with her, she was also sharing with him. And, since he was a superstar in the world of classical music, he was the one they cared about.

"I would like to answer that myself, if you don't mind."

Everyone turned toward the deep sound of Gerick's voice. The room buzzed at seeing him, but when he spoke there was an instant hush. He had total control over them, the type of control Ayn had dreamed of having. For the first time, Ayn fully understood how he must have felt when he told her he was tired of competing with her. Strange how time had reversed their roles. She had started out so much quicker and stronger than he had, but musical directors move up at a much slower pace, and Gerick had shot past her long ago. He'd achieved his glory, while she was still struggling for hers.

She would never be content to remain in his shadow, and she knew also that the odds against her fight had just increased. She would have to prove so much more now, or some would accuse her of reaching her peak only with Gerick's help. Suddenly she wished he'd never joined with ISO, but then they would never have gotten back together. But why did it have to happen now?

The rest of the interview was like a tennis match. Gerick would try to direct questions back to Ayn, she would answer, but the press would then turn back to Gerick with the next question. Outwardly Ayn appeared undisturbed by the chain of events; inwardly she was seething, and she could tell by the way Gerick looked at her that he knew she was upset.

Afterward, she discreetly excused herself and hurried from the room. She heard footsteps rushing after her but she didn't look back. Gerick finally fell into stride beside her. Ayn continued on as though he weren't there, not trusting herself to speak rationally.

"I didn't mean for it to go that way," Gerick said.

"But it did."

"I'm sorry, but it's your own fault."

"My fault?" she repeated, acting more astonished than she was.

He took her arm, stopping her abruptly. "Yes, your fault! Why in the hell did you announce I had joined your company?"

"Silly of me, wasn't it? I guess I was under the illusion that I—or the orchestra—was as important as you are. Apparently we're not."

Gerick shook his head. "Oh, Ayn, you know that's not true, not to the people who really matter. Your patrons and people who really *know* the arts have always known. However, if you're standing in a room full of headline-hungry reporters, then yes, I suppose I am more important. Or at least I make a flashier story."

Again Ayn was afraid to talk, afraid she'd lash out and say things she didn't really mean. Gerick stroked her cheek with his finger.

"Come on, let me see that smile I love."

Ayn turned her head away. "Please, I want to be alone. I need to think."

"I don't believe it! You're not just annoyed, you're angry at me, aren't you?"

"Yes."

"Why? I tried to give the attention back to you." She glared at him. "I don't want your charity."

"Charity!"

"Gerick, I've worked all my life for this moment, and I had to accept your handouts to get to say a word. Do you realize that I am not only the youngest conductor of an acclaimed orchestra, but also one of the first women ever to obtain such a position?"

"Yes, I do realize that—"

"But *they* don't!"

"Ayn, I understand what you're feeling—"

"How could you?"

His body became rigid with anger. "I went through it ten years ago, remember?"

Gerick placed his hands on her shoulders. "Ayn, don't let this come between us. Not again." She made no reply. "Come on, let's go someplace better suited to discuss this."

"No," she said softly, then added, "Benny's offered to drive me home."

Gerick's eyes burned with a white-hot fire. He stepped back as though she'd just slapped him. "Fine!" he said, then turned and walked away.

Chapter Six

$\mathcal{G}$erick walked past the sign, which read Rehearsal Closed to the Public. Then, doubt stopped his hand as he reached for the door. He hadn't been this nervous before confronting Ayn at the Metronome after a ten-year separation. So why should not seeing Ayn for a little over a month throw him into a sweat? Perhaps because there was no denying it now. He loved her; he always would. The problem was, things were so different from what he'd expected Even Ayn was different—better, but definitely different.

Looking around, he noticed the door to the director's room was ajar. ISO used an old theater hall for rehearsals and the control booth at the back of the house was the perfect answer. He could see her without being seen.

It took a moment for his eyes to adjust to the

127

blackness inside the tiny room beyond the glass wall. The theater was dark too. Only the stage lights were on, almost blinding as Gerick tried to focus. The musicians were in their seats and a few people were milling around the stage, but no one was at the podium. Then he saw her bent down at the edge of the stage talking to Hank, the assistant manager.

He watched as she straightened and walked back to her raised platform. In the absolute silence of the booth it was like watching a dream. She was a vision he could only admire from a distance without touching. Ayn rubbed her temple and he knew her next movement would be to drop her hand into the "ready" position. When she did, a hundred pairs of eyes fixed on her immediately.

What control, he thought, slamming his palm on the counter in front of him. He had played with every major orchestra around the world, yet few conductors had so much power without verbal threat.

"Good Lord, Gerick, you scared me half to death," Hank said, moving past him. "What on earth are you doing sitting here in the dark?"

Gerick shrugged as Hank turned on a dim light and spread an assortment of papers on the counter. He scratched his ear as he examined one in particular and Gerick leaned forward to resume his study of Ayn. Suddenly Hank frowned and threw his pencil down.

"Gerick, you're not supposed to be here!" he said almost in a whine. "What I mean is, it's okay for you to be here in this room, but . . . well, you're not even supposed to be in New York. I thought you were clearing up business on the West Coast?"

"I finished earlier than I expected," Gerick said, not offering that he'd actually wrapped up his affairs three weeks before and had spent the rest of the time at Jonathan's beach house thinking.

"Well, I'm glad you're back. Does Ayn know you're here yet?"

"No," Gerick said with a shake of his head.

Hank flipped the switch on the microphone. "I'll tell her."

"No," Gerick said, placing one hand over the mike and turning it off with his other hand. "Don't interrupt her while she's conducting."

Looking up, Hank's mouth dropped open. "Well, Holy Handel, I didn't realize they'd started up again. She'd bite my head off if I bothered her now." He turned a knob on the control panel and music flooded the room. "Why did you have the sound off? Did I disturb you or something?"

"No, the truth is, I didn't have time to adjust the volume. I'd just walked in."

Hank nodded, but Gerick knew he didn't really believe him. Gerick leaned forward and concentrated on listening to the melody, hoping to keep Hank from pondering too long on the strange violinist next to him.

"Beethoven?" Gerick asked. "Has there been a change in the program?"

"Yes, that's why I knew Ayn would be happy to hear you were back. She has some things to discuss with you." Hank blew at a strand of thin blond hair. "Believe me, it was not a pleasant job having to tell her you had some previous commitments to attend to."

It was a dirty trick, but Gerick had excused

himself from the rehearsal, thinking they both needed time apart. He'd hoped that absence would, indeed, make her heart grow fonder. It certainly had for him.

"You mentioned something about Ayn biting your head off. Has she been upset over something lately?" he asked, hoping she'd been as lonely as he was.

"Let's just say we've all been under a lot of pressure for the past month."

Gerick was disappointed that he couldn't get more out of the assistant manager, and yet, he was glad to know Hank wasn't the type to talk about other people. Gerick chuckled at his own childishness. If Ayn was upset by his absence, she certainly wouldn't say so to Hank, or to anyone for that matter.

"So, are you going to share the joke with me, or just sit there with that grin on your face?"

Gerick laughed. He liked Hank; in fact, he liked everyone he'd met with the ISO. "I was just wondering what it would be like to work under a woman." He raised an eyebrow. "A very rare phenomenon in my line of work."

Hank took a pack of gum from his shirt pocket and offered Gerick a piece. Gerick shook his head and watched as Hank unwrapped a stick and started chewing it before he responded.

"Well, they say there shouldn't be any difference between working for a female or a male musical director, but I say they're wrong."

He paused and chewed heavily on the gum. Gerick leaned on his elbow, trying to anticipate if Hank was about to stop being diplomatic and give his real feelings. A small part of Gerick hoped it would be so, for he'd finally realized that he would have to work under Ayn's direction and it was a bit frightening. It was not that she was a woman that bothered him. That was only an excuse one man would use with another. What did bother him was her knowledge of him. Ayn knew everything about him, not just as a lover but as a man. Other conductors stood in awe of him, at least enough not to cross him, but Ayn knew when he was bluffing.

Hank cracked the gum between his teeth. "You're going to have to watch her real close."

Gerick looked confused. "You mean I can't trust her?"

Suddenly Hank looked confused. "No, I don't mean that at all. That little lady would do anything for her musicians. That's why they love her so much, even though she's a perfectionist." He looked around as though someone might overhear his secret. "It's the way she moves, Gerick. You have to watch her extremely close."

"Her movements," Gerick repeated, drawing his brows together in mock concern.

"I don't know if all women conductors move with such grace, but Ayn does. If I was in the orchestra I'd forget to play a note and just watch her all day."

Gerick leaned back, locking his fingers behind his head. He couldn't help the smile that swept across his face. "Thanks, Hank, I'll remember to watch her—real close."

"No, no, no." The music had stopped and Ayn's voice flooded the control room.

Gerick sat up. "What's wrong? It sounded great to me."

Hank shrugged. "I told you she's a perfectionist."

Gerick thought Ayn looked very tired as she leaned forward on the podium to talk to the orchestra. He listened, hoping to gain a better insight into the professional woman he'd be working with for the next few months.

"Beethoven's *Pastoral* is one of his most popular symphonies. We've all heard it hundreds of times, right?" Everyone nodded in agreement. "It's a bittersweet melody that we could probably all play in our sleep, right?" Again they agreed. "Wrong!"

Gerick and Hank gave each other questioning looks before Ayn continued.

"I want you to do me a favor. I want you to forget your preconceived notions about the man and his music. Forget you've ever heard or played Symphony Number Six. I know it sounds impossible, but try, for me."

She paused, bringing her hands together in front of her face. "Now, picture the young man who loved being included in the Viennese aristocracy. Included by the sheer force of his personality and because no one could deny he was a musical genius." She smiled. "You've heard this all before, I know, but remember there was one thing he worshiped more than the fame and the parties. Beethoven was a man who deeply loved the outdoors."

Gerick leaned back. "She's a speech giver, like Jonathan."

"Not really," Hank corrected. "This is the first one I've heard."

Gerick rolled his eyes and tuned back in.

". . . and he felt he had to hide the fact that he

was losing his hearing. He wrote, 'For me there can be no recreation in the society of my fellows. . . . I must live like an exile.' He was angry and defensive and he became a surly recluse. It was during this period that he wrote the Fifth and Sixth symphonies."

She rocked on her heels and slipped her hands into the pockets of her skirt. "The Fifth is contrasting variations. He lulls the audience; then, in an exhilarating rush, he leaps forward. The momentum shatters all he's built, only to rebuild it in a triumphant image. *That* was the epitome of his struggle against the fates, not the Sixth Symphony.

"By the time he wrote the *Pastoral* he had come to terms with himself. Outwardly he remained a grouch, but inside, for a while, he was filled with joy and peace. The title says it all: 'Cheerful Impressions Awakened by Arrival in the Country.' Plain and simple. He had finally ventured back outdoors, and though he was almost totally deaf, he heard the delicate beauty of the rural life in his mind."

She paused, studying the faces of those listening to her. Her hands came from her pockets to help express her point. "It was not written as a bittersweet memory for himself, but to serve all the future generations. Because of the *Pastoral* we can close our eyes here, today, in Manhattan and visualize that countryside. We can see it all. From the first beams of sunlight on the fields to the quick thunder of the summer rain to the glorious finale—after the storm."

She sighed, waiting for a response from the orchestra members. No one spoke.

"Well, that is what I hope we'll be performing for Russia in December. Now, after that little speech, I think we should call it a day. See you tomorrow."

Hank began to gather his papers. "She's going to knock their socks off in Moscow."

"Do you really think so?" Gerick asked, wanting to believe it but afraid he was prejudiced.

"I know so! I've been in this business too long not to recognize what she has."

With every fiber of his being, Gerick prayed Hank was right. Then and only then would they have a chance to make it together.

"I've got to go tell her what a genius she is. Coming?"

Gerick shook himself from his daze. "No, not right now." He reached up and turned off the lights. He needed a moment alone to prepare himself again to face her. How on earth was he going to keep this a strictly professional relationship? "By the way, Hank, would you do me a favor and not mention that you saw me here?"

"Sure . . . ah, is there anything wrong? I mean, you're not having doubts about joining us now that Jonathan's out of the picture?"

"No, of course not. I'm just going through a bit of a personal crisis right now. Nothing to worry about; everything will work itself out." He shrugged. "Besides, I've never let my feelings interfere with my professionalism."

And, he thought sadly, neither does Ayn. He wondered if that was most of their problem. Perhaps they didn't love each other enough. He'd always heard that most people couldn't eat or sleep or work when they were in love. That never happened to them, however. They went right on as usual.

"What's wrong, can't decide which girl to take to the disco tonight?" Hank asked, trying to lighten the mood.

"Something like that," Gerick said, forcing a laugh as Hank left. Alone again, he sobered. Hank didn't take him seriously. No one did, except when he was performing. He'd intended to create the facade of a devil-may-care playboy, and he'd succeeded.

Gerick rubbed his hands over his eyes. Would they believe that the real Gerick Grier had loved only one woman in his entire life? Would they believe he was so obsessed with her that he couldn't stay away yet at the same time he was so scared of losing Ayn that he couldn't face her?

The rehearsal hall was emptying fast as Hank approached the stage. Ayn stood poring over the score when she heard him behind her. Turning, she hoped she didn't look too anxious.

"There you are. I was wondering where you'd gone to."

Hank jerked his head toward the back of the theater. "I was in the control room."

"So—did you hear?"

His face registered no emotion. "Every word."

"And . . . ?"

"And, I think they bought it."

"I know *they* bought it. But what I need from you, Hank, is your honest opinion on what the audience will think."

He rubbed his chin thoughtfully, then smiled. "They will love it."

She brought her hand up to her mouth to hide the full smile that couldn't be stopped. "Thanks, Hank. You're the greatest!"

"So are you, Ayn. We're lucky to have you." He glanced around. "Musicians can move faster than any other human beings when they're dismissed. There's not a soul in sight. If you're ready to go, I'll walk you out."

"No, I have a few more things to do around here first."

Hank grimaced. "How can you stand to hang around a deserted theater? It gives me the creeps."

Ayn laughed. "Except for the moment when I bring a song to life, this is the time I love the best. After the commotion dies and everyone's gone home."

"If you ask me, it's just plain spooky in here."

"Only the ghosts of melodies linger here." She looked around. "You know, it all began for me in a deserted hall very similar to this one. I was ten years old and my father took me to my very first concert— Forgive me," she said, snapping out of the past. "I didn't mean to rattle on like that."

Hank backed up and sat in a chair in the first row. "Neither one of us is leaving this place until you finish that story."

"It's of little significance to anyone but me."

"And me. As assistant manager it's my job to know certain things about you. I've found out that unlike Jonathan, who wanted to have dozens of people around him before a concert, you prefer to be alone with a cup of chamomile tea. I know the type of towels you want in your dressing room and if someone sends you lilacs, you cry. And I've discov-

ered that if there are children in the audience who
want to see you, they are to be given V.I.P. treat-
ment and brought backstage. Is it because of something that happened when you were a child? Come
on, Ayn, tell me what started it all.''

She sat on the edge of the stage, dangling her feet,
and was surprised at how natural it felt to talk to
Hank. ''My mother had recently died and, bless his
heart, my father was trying to spend time with his
daughter. I thought it was very astute of him to
choose music as a way to bring us closer. I loved
music. Later, I found out there was someone at the
concert that he wanted to see and to be seen with. I
didn't really mind, though; he'd always been a better
businessman than a father.'' Ayn stopped, realizing
she was telling more than she'd intended to. ''Are
you sure you want to hear all of this?''

Hank waved her on, then popped a fresh stick of
gum in his mouth.

''Anyway,'' she said, then let a sigh carry her back
through the years, ''there I was, alone in that huge
empty auditorium. I remember how I kept looking
around as I walked up the aisle. There was no one in
sight. Inside my head I was still hearing the music,
and finally, when I couldn't resist it anymore, I
stepped up on the podium. It was like stepping onto
a little piece of heaven.'' She brought her hands
together, tapping her fingers against her lips before
continuing.

''When I picked up the baton, all the exalted
feelings music had ever brought me seemed to come
together. In that instant I experienced the greatest
feeling of joy that I've ever known. Then I closed my
eyes and began to conduct the music I was hearing in

my mind. It was glorious. As though I'd been deaf all my life and could suddenly hear. That's how right it felt, but when I opened my eyes, *he* was standing there in front of me."

"Who was? Your father?"

"No," she said softly, reverently. "The conductor. I was so embarrassed I ran out of the concert hall, but I've never forgotten how he looked at me and smiled. It was as if he was saying, 'Yes, child, someday you'll belong on this podium.'"

She lifted her hands in a helpless gesture. "That's how it all started. From then on I was hooked and gave all my love and devotion to music. To this day my poor father doesn't understand me, but we've learned to accept each other for what we are."

Hank crossed his legs. "If you think you're going to get away with telling me that kind of a story without telling me who the conductor was, you've got another think coming."

Ayn stood. Slowly, she walked to the podium and ran her fingers over the smooth wood. It was such a wonderful memory and she couldn't or didn't want to stop talking about it, and besides, Hank was such an interested listener.

"I'm still waiting for the name of this hero," he said, grinning.

Ayn smiled. "That's exactly the way I thought of him. He became the hero of all my childhood fantasies. My friends were dreaming about rock and roll stars, but I was picturing a man with black hair that was just starting to gray at the temples. He's totally silver now, but he's still an extraordinarily handsome man."

Hank snapped his fingers. "Of course, I should have guessed sooner. It was Jonathan, right?"

Ayn smiled.

Hank laughed. "You know, for a minute, when you first described him, all I could see was Gerick."

Ayn's eyes grew wide at his statement. She'd managed not to think about Gerick for at least ten minutes, and Hank had to bring up the subject.

"Did I say something wrong?"

Ayn shook her head. "No, but maybe you're right. This place is kind of creepy. I'd better finish up and leave."

"Want me to wait?" he asked, standing.

"No," she said, waving him away. "I just have to make a few corrections on this score; then I'll be on my way. You go on."

Hank nodded and headed for the stage door. Ayn quickly made her note, then walked to the piano to retrieve her jacket from the bench. Something about the gleaming keys made her stop, then sit down. Without really thinking, she began to play. Her fingers rolled into the opening chords as naturally as her heart rolled into the image of Gerick playing the Rachmaninoff rhapsody at the beach house. She'd always thought it was the most poignant love song ever written. It began with the painfully sharp sadness of someone who thinks they will never see their one and only again. Then he's there and, elated, she runs to him. They embrace and kiss, knowing it will be the very last time they will be able to give of themselves. They must summon enough passion to sustain them through all eternity—for they know it can't last.

Slowing, he drifts away and she is alone again, with only his memory. In the last refrain she is smiling: his memory is enough.

Ayn pounded the keys violently. "It's not enough," she cried, dropping her head into her hands.

A one-man applause struck out from the dark theater, instantly stopping her release of pent-up tears. Without lifting her head she knew who her audience was. How dare he walk in when she was finally ready to have the cry she'd been promising herself ever since he'd left! Gerick was right. They had lousy timing.

When she did look up, he was standing in the shadows just beyond the circle created by the stage lights. She couldn't count the number of times she'd hoped he'd walk down that very aisle. The time had come but she still couldn't see him. She wondered if he was so self-assured that he could tease her from the shadows. Did he know she was aching to see him, or was he as afraid of the confrontation as she was?

Ayn willed herself not to look at his silhouette when she stood. Knowing he would have to come back to fulfill his contract, she'd rehearsed their meeting several times in her mind. In her script, though, she was never caught on the verge of tears. She was always poised and charming, sometimes even witty. At that moment, however, she could think of nothing to say except, "Hello, Gerick."

"Hello," he said quietly, the acoustics of the old hall carrying the rich tone of his voice with brilliant clarity. Her skin tingled as though he'd reached out across the distance and touched her.

"When did you get back in town?" she asked, then wished she'd worded the question differently. The last thing she wanted was for Gerick to think she was keeping tabs on him.

"I just got back into New York last night."

She wanted to be nasty and say that the gossip columnists were falling down on their job. His name hadn't been splashed all over the news this morning, but if she mentioned it he might suspect she had been reading to find out his whereabouts. She was, just as she had every morning since he'd left. Nothing had been mentioned about him from either coast the entire time he was gone.

Finally she offered a noncommittal, "Oh," and moved to the podium. Standing with her back to him, she could still feel his eyes watching her every movement and tried to appear preoccupied with closing up the score. "Too bad you couldn't have worked it into your busy schedule and gotten here early enough for the rehearsal." She was growing more sarcastic with each word and took a deep breath before continuing, "We've made some changes in the program and we were discussing them today."

"As a matter of fact, I was here and I heard everything that was said on this stage."

Ayn whirled to face where he stood. She glared in his direction. "You were here?" she asked, not bothering to hide her anger.

"In the control booth with Hank."

Her hands flew to her hips. "Why didn't you come down and join the orchestra, or is that too far beneath the Great Gerick Grier?"

"I thought it best if we saw each other alone," he

said, then stepped into the light. Seeing Gerick was like the thunder that followed lightning. No matter how Ayn tried to prepare herself for it, when the moment exploded before her, she quivered with excitement and awe. His eyes were melancholy when he added, "Besides, I lost my nerve at the door."

Ayn drew in her breath sharply and turned her back on him. No, she thought, don't let him be human, not now. Please not now. She didn't want to understand his side or to feel any compassion for him. She wanted to stay angry and hurt. If she didn't they'd fall back into each other's arms, and where could an embrace lead? It could only take them down a path that neither of them was ready to explore to the end.

She didn't hear him move, yet it didn't surprise her when she sensed Gerick was behind her. She saw his large hands pause a moment before coming to rest on her shoulders.

"Did you miss me?" he asked, sounding like a child who was unsure of his worth.

Ayn's heart melted. "More than you'll ever know," she said, turning and throwing her arms around his waist.

Gerick hesitantly placed one arm around her shoulder and then his other arm wrapped around her waist. He drew her close, so that her face rested against his chest. She could feel the rhythm of his heart and hers, counterrhythms trying to harmonize with each other.

"Oh, Ayn, my precious Ayn. How I've missed you."

She couldn't answer. Her throat was aching with emotions she didn't trust to release. She swallowed back the tears, for their embrace was not born of passion but of the need of two people who had shared the good times and the bad and had found that nothing was important unless it was shared with one another.

"I've given a lot of thought to us and our future together. I must admit, right now we're on very shaky ground." Ayn clung tighter to him. To ease her fears, he touched his lips to the silky softness of her hair and left a tender kiss. "We tried to pick up where we'd left off and it just can't be done after ten years. We've both changed and grown and we need to find out who and what we've become."

Ayn lifted her head and stared into the gentle blue of his eyes. She already knew what he'd become and she loved it. He stroked her hair, then eased her head back against his chest. As if reading her thoughts, he continued; "We need to discover these new people without letting desire color our opinions. I want to become your friend again."

"I'd like that—very much," she said softly.

They didn't move apart until the silence made it necessary.

Ayn felt like a sixteen-year-old on her first date, not knowing what to do next. She gave a quick, nervous smile. "I know you're right, Gerick, but how or where do we begin again?"

"Well, for starters, how about lunch? Are you free?"

She looked at her watch and gasped in horror. "Oh, my gosh, I'm supposed to meet Andrews in fifteen minutes."

Gerick grabbed her jacket and helped her into it. "Where are we supposed to meet Andrews?" he asked as they rushed toward the stage door. Hitting the locking bar, he held the door open for Ayn.

"The Russian Tea Room," she called over her shoulder as she hurried past him.

Gerick almost ran down the alleyway to catch up with her. Taking her hand, he pulled her on to match his strides. "We'd better get a cab," he said as they broke into the lunchtime crowd on the avenue. Still pulling her along, Gerick weaved through the mass of moving people until they reached the curb. After a few minutes they hailed a taxi. Once inside and the destination given, Gerick leaned back against the seat with a sigh.

Ayn glanced again at her watch. "We should just make it in time."

Gerick smiled. "Mind if I ask you something?"

"No, what?"

"Who's this Andrews fellow? I mean, even if we are supposed to be just friends, he might not appreciate me tagging along if this is a date." His eyes narrowed. "And if this is a date, then I may have to reconsider my stand on us remaining just friends."

Ayn laughed at the absurd thought. "Andrews is definitely not a date. It's strictly business."

"Good!" Suddenly he grabbed the passenger loop to keep from falling on Ayn as the driver rounded a corner. "So, what sort of business will we be discussing at lunch?"

"Bob Andrews is a professional manager from my publishing firm," she offered, waiting to see Gerick's reaction.

He nodded. "If I recall, the last time I saw you, you were mad because I'd dared to play your blasted symphony. Now, you're trying to get it published. Talk about from one extreme to the other."

"Well, you said you really liked it, so I thought I'd give it a try. You did like it, didn't you?"

"I loved it."

"I hope Andrews feels the same as you do," she said, biting on her lower lip.

"He will or he's a fool."

"Thank you," Ayn said, touching his arm. Then, thinking the gesture was too intimate, she dropped her hand to the seat.

Gerick looked at her hand, then lifted his gaze to hers. "It's not going to be easy, is it?"

Ayn shook her head and looked away. They remained silent until they reached the corner of Seventh Avenue and Fifty-seventh Street. Stepping from the cab, Ayn glanced at the building across from her. She felt that little tug at her heart that every musician feels each time they see Carnegie Hall.

Gerick took her hand and darted across the street between the slow-moving traffic. When they stepped on the curb, he looked up and almost blanched. "So, that's what had you mesmerized."

They both stared for a moment as if in worship. "No matter how many times I see it, I still get goose bumps," Ayn said, rubbing her arms.

"When I was a kid and all the other boys were worried if they'd ever grow any taller than their girlfriends, all I could think about was getting to Carnegie Hall."

Ayn nodded; she understood. "I rarely dated a guy more than once because I always made them bring me here for a concert. I was known as Ayn 'The Bore' Remington."

He held out his hand. "Meet Gerick 'The Wimp' Grier."

She shook his hand. "The Wimp? *You?*"

"I was either practicing, taking lessons or working to pay for more lessons, and in my neighborhood that made you a wimp."

They'd stopped shaking hands, but Gerick still held her hand firmly in his. "We're kindred spirits, you and I."

Ayn looked at him sadly. "I think star-crossed lovers is a more fitting description."

His eyes denied it, but his sigh didn't. "Perhaps you're right." He released his hold. "Let's go. We don't want to keep Andrews waiting."

They covered the few steps to the tea room in silence. Ayn hated herself as they stepped into the brass-trimmed revolving door. She couldn't understand why she'd said what she had. It had been so lovely calling up visions from the past. She too had always felt they were kindred spirits, from their very first meeting.

"I'll tell the maître d' we're here. What name is the reservation under?"

"Andrews, and I don't see him waiting out here, so he's probably already started on the bread basket."

She leaned against the cloak room wall and watched Gerick work his way through the line of waiting people. He moved with a sleekness and a grace that would be more natural for a dancer than a concert violinist. He was so attractive, and yet it hadn't been his good looks that had drawn her to him when they'd first met.

She remembered how excited she'd felt that night. Her recommendation had been accepted at Juilliard, and to celebrate, she'd gone to hear the Philharmonic. The lights had just darkened in Avery Fisher Hall when there was a rustling in the seat next to her. At the time she wasn't positive, but she thought she remembered a round middle-aged man sitting on her right. When she glanced at the man beside her, the silhouetted figure had become tall and slim. Not long after the concert began, he leaned over and whispered, "Isn't he magnificent?"

Normally she would have been irritated, but his voice was intriguing and sincere, so she answered. Then she discovered he was talking about the soloist and she about the conductor. They continued commenting throughout the performance. To avoid bothering the others around them, he would lean extremely close and cup his hand to her ear. His whispers dealt totally with music, yet there was a strange feeling of intimacy in the way he spoke.

For the first time in her life, Ayn could hardly wait for the symphony to end. She was dying to see the man next to her. Sure that someone who complemented her thoughts as he did must look like Quasimodo, she was pleasantly relieved when she saw Gerick. During intermission they found out more and more about each other. In spite of their vastly different upbringings, when they talked of their dreams, their ideals and their music, an affinity formed instantly. Ayn tried to explain away her attraction to him as being only the attraction of one

musician to another, but even then she recognized
the lie for what it was. She knew hundreds of
musicians and none had affected her as Gerick did.

"A penny for your thoughts," Gerick said, bringing her back to the present.

"I was just thinking about how we met. It was
fate, or kismet or something."

"It was all the money I had in my pocket."

"What?"

He laughed. "I hate to burst your bubble, but it's
true. I was sitting a couple of rows behind you and
decided I had to talk to you. So I caught the guy next
to you in the aisle and paid him to change seats with
me when the lights went out." He grinned like a
small boy. "I had to meet you."

"I can't believe you never told me that."

"I was afraid you'd look at me as you are now."
Again he laughed. "That was the reason I couldn't
take you out for an after-the-concert drink. I was flat
broke. The guy next to you knew he had a lovesick
fool on his hands and he didn't agree on an amount
until I ran out of offers."

Ayn smiled fully, then quickly drew her lips
together. Gerick rested his hand on the wall directly
above her head, then leaned close to her. Ayn raised
her hand and placed it against his chest, but she
lacked the conviction to stop him as he moved closer
and closer. Gently, he kissed her dimple. For a
moment she couldn't breathe. Longing erupted inside her and sent molten desire through her veins.

His name was a high-pitched plea. "Gerick,
please."

"Yes," he growled, his lips seeking the softness of
hers.

"Someone will see us."

He froze momentarily, then straightened. His massive shoulders rose and fell with hurried breaths as he remained alarmingly close to her. Ayn could feel the heat of his stare and she looked up into the face she loved. His voice was still throaty with need when he spoke. "Don't *ever* smile like that again." Then, mask in place over his feelings, he turned to face the maître d' as he motioned for them to follow him to their table.

Ayn felt drained and was glad when Gerick slid his arm around her waist. She patted his hand in thanks, and he grabbed her fingers. Glancing up, she shook her head. "I thought we're supposed to be just friends?"

He looked directly ahead, smiling at the restaurant full of people. "I told you it wasn't going to be easy." He waved to a fellow musician. "This is a very poor choice for a nice, quiet business lunch."

"Andrews picked it. He loves the Wednesday special."

"So does everyone else in New York, apparently," he said, teeth clenched into a permanent smile.

Sprinkled through the forest-green-and-red interior were a couple of movie producers, a Tony Award–winning director/choreographer and a few ministars of stage and screen. Less obvious to the delighted tourists among them was a mixture of columnists, novelists and critics.

The sight of the two of them together caused an audible stir among the patrons. When Ayn smiled at Babs Thompson she could almost see the headline written across the columnist's brow. "Grier Scores with New Conductor."

Andrews was as shocked as the others and dropped a piece of dark bread on his plate. He stood to greet them at the booth. "Aynnie," he drawled, giving away his midwestern roots. "How good to see you and—" He turned to Gerick and feigned surprise. "Bust my britches if it isn't Gerick Grier. I'm delighted."

Gerick offered his hand. "Bob, isn't it? Bob Andrews?"

"Please, just Andrews, everyone calls me that."

In an almost magical flick of the wrist he produced his card.

Ayn slid into the booth between the two men. "I hope you don't mind that I invited Gerick to join us?"

"Aw, you know me better than that. The more the merrier, I always say, right, Aynnie?"

"Right," she said, steeling herself for the inevitable. It came right on cue, the approving slap on the back. She saw Gerick tense and her eyes sent out the message that it was all right.

Suddenly Andrews stood. "Excuse me a minute, will you all? Some critter just sauntered in and I've got to say howdy." He started to walk away, then stopped. "I've already ordered. The waiter will be back in a sec. I recommend the Siberian *pelmeny*, Aynnie. It's mighty good."

Gerick looked at her in distress. "He's some out-of-work actor that you hired to put on a show for me. Isn't he?"

She shook her head. "No, he's for real. Honest."

"Shucks, ma'am," Gerick mimicked. "You don't expect me to believe that, do you?"

"Andrews is the best PM around, as strange as it

may seem. When it comes to music he could sell anything."

Gerick leaned forward and shook his finger in her face. "If he slaps you again like you're his old drinking buddy, I swear, I'll deck him."

"No, Gerick," she said, then a laugh burst from her. "If he calls me Aynnie one more time, then you can deck him." She smiled and bit her lip as Andrews sat down again.

After the meal a waiter in a red cossack shirt began to clear the table. It was then that Ayn mentioned that they'd discussed everything in the music business except her symphony.

"Wait!" Andrews almost shouted. "Aynnie, aren't you going to finish your chicken Kiev?"

"It's a little too rich for me today."

Andrews snatched the plate from the waiter's hand. "No use letting good food go to waste, I always say."

"There's another thing you always say," Ayn said boldly. "'Classical music is the kind that we keep hoping will turn into a tune,' right?"

"No, Kin Hubbard said it; I just repeat it. I told you before I agreed to look at it that our firm does very few classical scores."

She'd had plenty of time during the meal to prepare herself for his answer. All that remained was to hear it said. "Does that mean you're not going to publish and promote it?"

"Yes, ma'am." His face was an apology.

She leveled an exaggerated look at Gerick and mouthed, "Deck him."

Gerick choked on his wine and brought the glass down on the table with a thud.

"You got to watch those crazy cossack bartenders. They mix some pretty powerful concoctions," Andrews offered, then turned to Ayn. "Darlin', it's hard to peddle classical stuff, especially new compositions. Why don't you write another Broadway musical? That would sell."

"Because I want to write symphonies."

"Aynnie, it's just like you said a minute ago. People want a tune, something they can hum along with."

"What about Beethoven's Fifth Symphony?" Ayn asked. Gerick started to hum the beginning phrase, then broke into another piece, which Ayn named. "Or his Ninth Symphony?" Again Gerick switched tunes.

Andrews clapped twice without enthusiasm. "You two should work up an act. That was very cute, but I'm still not convinced that enough interest can be created by a new and as yet unproven piece."

Ayn started to continue her arguments, but Gerick cut her short.

"Is that what you want? A proven piece?"

Andrews picked up the empty bread basket and motioned for a refill to a passing waiter. Turning his attention back to Gerick, he smiled. "Exactly, son."

"Then I suggest you have your legal department start drawing up the contract, because *The City* will be previewed by Christmas."

Ayn looked up in surprise, a reaction that Andrews didn't miss.

"Now, son, this preview has to be met with favorable reviews, and be performed by a major orchestra in a major music city."

Gerick took Ayn's hand and pulled her from the

booth as he slid out. "The Interurban Symphony Orchestra, Moscow. Good enough?"

The fork Andrews held was waved suspiciously toward them. "If Moscow likes it, you've got a deal."

Ayn ended the luncheon with polite salutations, and she and Gerick walked triumphantly through the restaurant. At the door, Ayn placed her hand on Gerick's arm to stop him. "Thank you, but I prefer to fight my own battles."

"I know, but it's not just your battle. It's a battle for all of us in classical music. How can we get new, fresh material if no one will believe in new composers?"

"I understand, but the point still remains. If I don't make it on my own, I don't make it. I don't want anyone to say I made it because you—"

"Ayn, what were you going to do?"

She closed her eyes for a moment. "I was going to do the same thing."

"Then why are we standing here arguing when we could be working on the score?"

"Do you really think it's ready to premier?"

He grinned. "We have six weeks to make it ready."

She stood on her toes and pecked his cheek. "Thanks, friend."

Chapter Seven

*N*ovember 20. Ayn ripped the page from her desktop calendar a day early. She'd stared at the date all morning, but couldn't pinpoint what bothered her about it. Still acting on impulse, she wadded the paper and threw it toward the trash basket. Naturally, she missed the receptacle and the twisted ball fell at Gerick's feet.

She knew it was him without looking up. Since their vow to become "just friends," she'd studied his feet many times to avoid looking into his eyes.

"Come in," she offered, although he was obviously already inside the small room. "What can I do for you?"

He bent and picked up the crumpled paper before easing his tall frame into one of the uncomfortable office chairs. She couldn't help feeling resentment toward his relaxed attitude, knowing she must look frazzled. Gerick tossed the ball in the air twice before she decided he wasn't going to talk.

She made her irritation obvious when she gave a deep sigh, but he continued to act as though she were the intruder to be ignored. It was a week until their departure for Russia and she didn't have time to play games. Disgusted, she began to scour the desk trying to remember what she'd been doing before he came in. Nothing came to mind.

"Is there something I can do for you?" she snapped.

"Nope," he answered, then tossed the paper high. Suddenly, he snatched it in midair and leaned forward to make his point. "But, there is something *I* can do for *you.*"

"Unless you brought my secretary back from the Bahamas, I seriously doubt it."

He jerked his thumb toward the outer office. "I take it the temporary is not working out well?"

"Let's put it this way: I'm giving her until Friday to figure out that the flashing line is the one that's ringing."

"That bad, huh?"

The phone rang and Ayn reached for it. Gerick's fingers wrapped around her wrist, halting her movement. Surprised, she looked up.

"Let her figure it out," he said. "I have something I want to discuss with you." With a sweep of his forearm he shoved the clutter to one side of her desk. Half sitting on the corner, he leaned close. "Let me take you away from all of this." He pulled her hand to his chest. "Come with me to the Casbah."

She laughed. "I'll have to take a raincheck on that one."

"I'm offering to take you to the sin city of the world and be intimate with you, and you're taking a raincheck?"

For the first time in six weeks she looked into his eyes. More than anything she wanted to see a cue that his suggestion held a hint of his true feelings. She did see hope in his gleaming blue stare, but she wasn't sure if it might be the reflection from her own eyes. The past few minutes had been the longest period of time they'd spent alone since the luncheon at the Russian Tea Room. She'd agreed at the time that what they were doing was the most logical and mature way of handling their relationship, but her opinion had changed over the last several weeks.

All the logic in the world couldn't erase the fact that they'd once shared a love and a life that had made them one. What was worse, the memory of that love was no longer a decade away, but only a couple of months ago. Pretending to know him casually was a strain. It felt as though a part of herself had attempted to strike out on its own, leaving a strange void.

"I'm serious, Ayn. You're working too hard. You need a break. How about a picnic lunch in Central Park?"

"Who should we invite to go with us?" she asked, crossing her fingers for the right answer.

"Absolutely no one. There's only room in the hansom for two."

She uncrossed her fingers, thankful that he was ready to move their relationship forward again. As he kissed her hand, Ayn saw a movement in the doorway. She leaned around and gave a questioning look to the bright-eyed girl who dared to call herself a secretary.

"Yes, Francine?"

"Excuse me, Miss Remington, but do you have an overdue book?"

"I beg your pardon?"

"The call, it's from the library and the only time I ever get a call is if I have an overdue book, so I thought—"

"I can assure you that's not why they're calling. Take a message, please." Ayn shook her head as she watched the girl leave. Then her thoughts became cohesive and she snatched her hand from Gerick. "Francine, wait!"

The pert face reappeared. "I took the message, just like you said."

Ayn sighed. "Was it from Helen?"

"Why yes, how'd you guess?"

Gerick's back was to the door and he didn't try to hide his amusement. Ayn gave him a warning glare, then turned back to Francine and explained politely. "Helen is *our* librarian. The orchestra has its own library for all our scores. Never mind, I'll call her back." Ayn rolled her eyes as she buzzed the library's extension. "This will just take a minute. I called her earlier about a bad turn for the cellos. She was going to have the section rewritten by tomorrow. Apparently something else has come up."

"Make it snappy," he said, juggling the paper wad from hand to hand. "Remember, the Casbah awaits." He glanced around to verify they were still alone. "By the way, who is Francine related to?"

"Hank. How'd you guess?"

"Call it male intuition."

Helen answered and Ayn spoke into the mouth-piece. "What's up?" She ran her hand through her hair. "What? No, no, not the Beethoven piece. The problem was on page one-thirty-seven of my symphony, *The City*. . . . I'm sorry, Helen, I'm sure it was my fault. I probably did say the *Pastoral*. Forgive me?" She slumped back in the chair. "I know, I've been working too hard. I just got that speech five minutes ago"—she glanced up, her hand reaching out to touch Gerick's—"from my best friend."

His fingers closed around the tips of hers and he smiled as though his greatest wish had just been granted. She smiled too, thinking that every lonely night she'd spent was worth the wait just to see him so happy. She looked away from Gerick, but not before feeling the warmth of a blush on her cheeks. It was the blush of a woman who'd just seen the unselfishness of a man's love for her. Helen's voice drew her back to reality.

"Yes, I'm still here . . . when? Tomorrow? Oh, Helen, you are a miracle worker. Yes, I promise to get some rest." Again she looked up. "As a matter of fact, I'm starting this afternoon. Thanks, see you later."

"Did you really mean that?" He stood and leaned, palms on the desk.

She felt embarrassed at revealing how deeply she cared for him, but there was no sense denying it. "Yes," she answered softly.

Again their eyes met, but only for an instant. The deep baritone of Benny Williams assaulted them from the doorway.

"What luck!" he said, clapping his hands together and rubbing them triumphantly. "I needed to talk to both of you and here you are, together."

"Come in, Benny," Ayn said, watching Gerick from the corner of her eye. He had picked up a pen and was writing something on her calendar pad.

Benny joined them at the desk as Gerick capped the pen and dropped it back in the mug inscribed with the words "I Love a Gershwin Tune . . ."

"Well," Gerick said, facing Benny. "What does our illustrious public relations man need to speak with the two of us about?" Ayn glanced at the note Gerick had scrawled. "Memo: Fire Benny."

She tried not to laugh as the short man offered, "It'll just take a minute."

Ayn motioned them to be seated and wondered if Benny caught the disgusted look on Gerick's face.

"I've been on the phone with some of the press people about next Friday night and—"

Ayn held up her hand. "Next Friday night? What about next Friday night?"

Benny shot a cautious look toward Gerick. "You didn't tell her?"

Gerick shrugged. "I thought *you* did."

Ayn looked from one to the other, then back. Her scrutiny was interrupted by the return of the secretary. "What is it now, Francine?"

"I need to file these," the young girl answered, waving a stack of papers in the direction of a large cabinet beside Ayn's desk.

"Go ahead. Now, gentlemen, what is going on next Friday night that neither of you has bothered to tell me about?"

Gerick stood. "How about if I explain it over lunch?"

"How about let's sit down and explain it now or there may be no lunch."

"It's quite simple, really," Benny started. "You know that snazzy disco Gerick frequents a lot?"

"Used to frequent a lot," Gerick interjected with a sheepish smile.

"It seems when they read that Gerick was going to tour Russia, well, they decided to have a going-away party for him. Oh, and the rest of the orchestra too. You know, one of those theme parties they're famous for?"

Ayn glared at Gerick. The playboy who loved to dance till dawn was a side of Gerick she'd forgotten existed. It suddenly occurred to her that while she'd been home, alone and worrying if they'd make it beyond friendship, he'd probably been dancing away his cares.

The phone rang, and in the tension-filled room, its shrill bell sounded like an alarm.

"I'll get it," Benny said, reaching across the clutter of her desk.

Ayn continued to stare at Gerick, not knowing whether to be angry or hurt.

Gerick smiled. "It's just a small get-together."

Francine leaned on the open drawer of the file cabinet. "A small get-together? Did you see those fancy invitations they sent out? Real ritzy looking."

Ayn lifted her eyebrow. "Invitations?"

"We don't need them," Gerick said, pointing to her and himself. "We're sort of like the guests of honor."

Ayn shook her head. *"We're* sort of like not going."

"Aw, come on, Ayn, it'll be fun."

Benny held the phone out. "It's Jonathan."

Ayn grabbed the receiver from him, but Benny's voice yelled over her shoulder, "Tell her she has to go."

She motioned them all to be quiet. "Jonathan, how's Florida?"

The familiar sound of his voice made her smile. "You have to go! Now, where does Benny want you to go?"

"Never mind. When are you coming home?"

"Three days, six hours, twenty-seven minutes and fifteen seconds."

"I thought you were having a great time letting your sister nurse you back to health and getting to know her darling kids?"

"That was the last report. It is now my sister the nag and her brats. Besides, a person can only take so much of this clean, sunny air." He kept talking, but Ayn couldn't hear the rest of his conversation. She was distracted by Benny talking with Francine, and Gerick who was playing with his paper wad again.

"I'm sorry, Jonathan, my office is full of people and I didn't hear you."

"It wasn't important. I'll call you tonight."

"That won't be necessary. I'll run them out."

She watched as Gerick placed one hand behind his back and pitched the paper ball over his head. The date had nagged at her; then Gerick's persistently playing with it irritated her even more. Ayn lunged past him, almost dropping the receiver. She grabbed the plaything from him and placed it on the desk. Leveling a stern look at him, she defied him to touch it again.

"Please," Jonathan said, "don't bother. Besides, I just noticed it's time for my tea. Say, shouldn't you be on your way to your lecture?"

Ayn slapped her forehead. "Good gosh, I forgot all about it. Thanks. Jonathan, I'll have to run. Call me later."

She hung up and began opening and closing drawers while scooping up the things she needed. "You'll have to excuse me. I have an appointment that completely slipped my mind."

"But what about Friday night?" Benny asked as she skirted the desk.

"We'll discuss it later." She glanced at Gerick. "Much later."

Rushing from the room, she heard Benny pleading. "You have to make her come. I told the press."

Gerick's footsteps sounded in the tiled hall behind her; then he fell into stride beside her. "Aren't you forgetting something?"

"I said we'll discuss it later."

He took her arm and pulled her to a stop. "Hang the party. I'm talking about you and me, today, Central Park and a picnic."

Her thoughts tumbled over the mass of confusion of the past few minutes, and she pressed her fingertips to her temple. She remembered the plans they'd made, plans she would now have to break. "I'm sorry, I can't today. Can we make it another time?"

"Are you really mad about the disco? If you are, I'll cancel the whole thing."

She touched his lips to stop him. "In there, yes, I was upset. Here, alone with you, I understand and I'm not mad. Really. It's a going-away party for a very important man."

"And a very important lady," he added, running the tip of his finger down the bridge of her nose. "I want to show you off to my friends. That's the only reason I agreed to it."

"I'll be there, but right now I have to be somewhere else." She started toward the door. Gerick blocked her path by extending his arm across the entrance.

"I'll go with you, then afterward we can . . ." His eyes finished the sentence.

"It's business and it may take a couple of hours. Besides, it's something I feel I must do on my own."

He dropped his arm and she hurried out the door and to the curb. He followed her slowly, thoughtfully. She stopped trying to hail a cab and walked back to him. Looking up into his face, she couldn't resist tracing his contours with her fingers. "Is *today* that important to you?"

He nodded, catching her hand with his. "But not important enough to ask you to stop this secret mission of yours." A taxi slipped to the curb beside them. "Go on, the Casbah's not very pretty this time of year anyway."

She hesitated, but he opened the door and urged her inside. Closing the door, he leaned in the window and kissed her cheek. Then he withdrew the wadded paper from his jacket. Straighten it out, he handed the calendar page to her.

A horn blasted angrily at them and the driver

pulled away. Gerick shoved his hands in his pockets and watched her leave. Through the rear window he saw her turn suddenly, her face sad with regret. She'd finally remembered November 20 was the anniversary of the day they'd met. With a squeal of tires, another taxi stopped beside him.

"Taxi, Mac?"

Gerick looked up, stunned. "What? No . . ." Then he thought. "Wait, yes!" He jumped in the back seat.

"Where to?"

"Follow that cab."

The driver placed his arm on the edge of the seat and turned to better see Gerick. "You've got to be kidding."

Gerick waved a twenty-dollar bill at the man.

The driver turned around and floored the accelerator. "Hold on, Mac, we're about to play TV detective."

"Don't get close enough for them to see us," Gerick cautioned as they eased through the less congested West Side traffic. Rounding a corner, Gerick immediately recognized the dingy street. "Whoa," he said, leaning forward to watch Ayn's cab.

"You think they're going to stop here?" the driver asked, studying the buildings for something he could identify.

"It's just a hunch," Gerick said, then smiled as the taxi braked and Ayn got out. "A very good hunch."

He paid his driver generously, then stepped out. Ayn was just disappearing into a brick building down the block, but Gerick decided it was best to keep his distance. He crossed the street and walked along the same path he'd traversed thousands of times in his youth.

Gerick studied the arched entrance across the street. How many times had he walked through those very doors into the High School of Performing Arts? For a moment he could almost see the young, gangling boy hesitating at the curb. He relived the boy's mixture of fear and anticipation. The fear was born of the realization that until that moment, only he had known he was destined to be somebody of worth. Even his mother had faced so many disappointments in her own life that she had only prepared him for failure. As with most mothers, she wanted to protect him from the hurt she'd known, but the boy had always known he wouldn't fail. Deep inside he'd believed he had something special, and from the minute he'd drawn a bow over the strings on a violin, he'd understood what that special talent was.

That first day was scary, though. The boy understood that once he entered the school, others would know and he couldn't turn back. They would see his ability and they would challenge his ambition. Blue eyes bright with determination, the boy remained outside, and the young man entered the school and began to live his dream.

Gerick shook the vision from his mind and returned to the present. This was *his* past, not hers. What was Ayn doing there? She'd never gone to a public school in her life. He realized he could speculate all day and still not come up with the correct answer. The only way was to ask her, directly. But did he have the right to confront her? She had said this was something she needed to do on her own.

He balled his fists and shoved them into the pockets of his jacket. Damn, she was a mystery. Straightening, he took one last look at the orange brick building, then walked away.

Halfway down the block he stopped. The words "Honesty, even if it hurts" chanted inside his head. Stubbornly Gerick turned and headed back to the school. He paused just inside the door as a feeling of nostalgia overcame him. Stepping beneath a white cupcake light, which was suspended from the pressed-tin ceiling, he remembered imagining it being his first spotlight. Gerick wondered if the students would lose some of their drive when the school moved uptown to share facilities with Lincoln Center. No, probably not. Kids seemed more affluent nowadays. Even the poor kids had more exposure to the arts than his generation had had.

Again he freed himself of the memories, then hurried up the slate stairs. His instincts carried him directly to the orchestra hall. No one was there. His feet knew it almost before his brain registered the thought, and he headed for the auditorium. He slipped into a seat near the back and listened to Ayn's lecture.

Gerick was amazed at how easily she kept the interest of the kids without talking down to them. Even when the questions and answers started, it was obvious she respected them as musicians. She pointed to a boy who looked as though he should be playing ball instead of clarinet. "Todd, isn't it?"

The boy nodded. "I hope you won't take this

wrong, Miss Remington, but why does an orchestra need a conductor?"

"Yeah," another chimed in. "We can all read music and count."

An embarrassed laugh giggled through the crowd. Ayn laughed too.

"That's a very good question. I used to wonder the same thing. Then one day I saw one of those 'Omnibus' shows with Leonard Bernstein." She paused and sighed. "I'm sure none of you are even old enough to remember the series, but he gave a most effective demonstration. At the opening he was conducting a Brahm's symphony. Then he walked away from the podium. For a while the orchestra continued; then slowly you began to hear them slipping out of synchronization. A conductor keeps the rhythm consistent."

One of the percussionists spoke up.

"It seems as though some conductors set themselves up as gods or something. I mean, if an orchestra is good, it's the conductor who gets all the praise."

"I assure you, Clint, I've never thought of myself as a god. However, if I can pull a hundred individuals together and teach them to interpret a piece with one solitary will, then I deserve recognition."

A towhead lifted his bow to signal his question. "Isn't it true that a conductor has to hear two different things at the same time? You know, what is being played and what is about to happen a moment later?"

Ayn smiled, and Gerick knew she was thrilled with the boy's knowledge. "You're right, Jess. If I'm not showing on my upbeat how the very next note should be played, then it's too late." She held up her hand to stop their questions as she continued. "There isn't a conductor alive who can make you play, but a truly great conductor can and must make you *want* to play. My job is to create a desire within you to have a passionate affair with the music.

"Just as two people in love must share one feeling, so must we. Our breathing, our movements, even our pulse must react simultaneously. Then and only then will we become one with our music and communicate our feelings to the audience. It is when this emotion is shared by all of us that the most unique of life's experiences occurs, pure love exists. After all, what is music if not a reflection of the best life has to offer?"

There was a moment of silence until Jess started to clap. Everyone joined in, but then the bell sounded. Gerick watched how the kids surrounded her and seemed reluctant to leave. Finally the teacher began to usher them out. The towhead hung back for a while, but was just about to leave when Ayn saw him.

"Jess, I'd like to talk with you," she called.

Gerick sat watching her, admiring her, loving her. He thought it must be rare to love someone on so many levels. He loved what she was personally, physically and professionally.

She was looking at the boy as they moved up the aisle toward Gerick. "I'm serious, Jess. I know we can work it out. I want you at Tanglewood next summer, if it's what you want."

"Oh, yes, Miss Remington. I want it more than anything."

"Good, I've—" She stopped suddenly, seeing Gerick. Her face was both shocked and relieved. "I'm glad you're here," she called to him.

The boy shuffled his books to show his awkwardness at the situation.

"Oh, excuse me," Ayn said. "Gerick Grier, I'd like you to meet Jess Jones. Someday he will be my replacement. Jess, this is Gerick Gr—"

"He needs no introduction, ma'am." The boy offered his hand to Gerick. "I can't believe I'm standing here with the two of you. It's like I've died and gone to heaven."

Ayn patted his hand. "I have your number, Jess, and as soon as we get back from Moscow, I'll be in touch."

The boy appeared to float out of the auditorium. "Keep practicing," Ayn called after him.

"I don't know if Jess is good or not, but he'll make it," Gerick said. "I saw that look in his eyes."

"I've been giving a series of talks here, and over the last couple of weeks I've seen *that look* a lot. Apparently this place specializes in it."

"Ayn, what was so blasted secret about coming here that you felt you couldn't tell me?"

She shrugged. "It seems silly now, but the original reason I volunteered for this was because of you. I thought perhaps I'd come to understand you better if I knew more about where you came from."

Gerick stared at her a moment. He wanted to take her and hold her and make her promise never to leave him. Though he knew the time wasn't right for him to demand a commitment from her, he still wanted to ask her for one. The nervous look that crossed her face only registered with Gerick when she turned and hurried from the room.

He rushed after her. "Ayn," he called in a hushed tone so as not to draw attention from the classrooms. She didn't look back and he realized she'd taken his silence for ridicule. He caught her and pinned her against the wall with his body.

"Look at me," he ordered. The curtain of lashes lifted, revealing the velvet brown of her eyes. Gerick fought to control the passion she stirred in him.

"I don't think it was silly at all. I thought it was touching, very touching."

She smiled seductively and the scent of her perfume permeated the air around them. "Do you think we can still make it to the Casbah today?"

He felt himself weakening and drawing closer to her lips. "That depends," he breathed the words heavily. "We still have some unfinished business."

"What?"

"This," he answered, his lips already tasting hers.

Suddenly something was rapping on Gerick's shoulder. Then a matronly voice ordered, "Break it up, kids. No fraternizing in the halls."

A jazzed up version of "Midnight in Moscow" was blaring from the speakers surrounding the dance floor. Above Ayn's head three twirling mirrored balls were spotlighted by a rainbow of laser lights. Below her feet multicolored lights danced on and off in time with the music. The noise and the neon combined to make her feel dizzy and giddy. It had to be the lights; she'd only had one White Russian. The manager had really gone overboard in decorating the disco with a cossack theme, and she couldn't refuse his insistence that she try the drink at least once.

Beyond the dance floor the club was decorated like a huge ice palace, but the closeness of too many bodies ruined the effect. The heat felt more like a sultry night on the bayou than a frosty night on the Baltic.

Ayn lifted the hair off her neck and smiled at Hank. He chomped his gum twice in response. She was figuring how many more members of the crew she'd have to dance with before she could spend time with Gerick, when suddenly he was beside her.

"May I cut in?" he shouted above the din.

Hank nodded and rumba-stepped himself through the crowd. Gerick's arm circled her waist and he pulled her tight, slowing their movements.

"This is supposed to be a fast dance," Ayn teased.

"You look horrible."

"Thanks," she shouted sarcastically.

He leaned closer so he wouldn't have to yell so much. "I mean, you look exhausted. Why don't we get out of here?"

"That's the nicest thing you've ever said to me."

Off the floor, smoke hung like a dense fog and trapped the heady blend of perfumes. Ayn's eyes watered and she almost didn't see Jonathan until he passed them.

"Hey, Maestro, I haven't had the chance to talk to you all evening."

"Later, dear. Francine and I are going to dance." He grinned and followed the girl to the dance floor.

Ayn frowned. "He shouldn't be out there."

"Relax, mother," Gerick teased, gathering her wrap from their table and draping it over her shoulders. "The doctor wants him to stay active."

Gerick's hand slid around her waist and he guided her toward the exit.

"I'm not that tired if you want to stay longer," she lied.

"We've made our appearance for the press and public. Now I want some time alone with you."

"I'm glad," she said as they stepped into the cool night air. She breathed in the autumn crispness. "What a lovely night."

Gerick murmured his agreement as he stepped to the curb to signal his limousine, which was waiting down the street.

Ayn touched his arm. "Why don't you let him go? We can walk back. It's not that far to my place."

Gerick gave instructions to the driver, then straightened and offered his arm to her. As they walked in silence, Ayn was doubly aware of everything around her. The heavy traffic sounds from Times Square, only a block away, played like a symphony in her ears. The air tickled her skin with a chill that made Gerick's arm around her shoulder feel like a warm blanket on a cold morning. She snuggled against him, their bodies moving in a simultaneous rhythm. With his left hand, Gerick pointed toward the sky. Hanging beside the silvery top of the Chrysler Building was a beautiful full moon.

Suddenly Gerick stopped, a perplexed look on his face. Ayn moved to stand in front of him. "What's wrong?"

He smiled down at her. "Oh, nothing really. I just

realized I'd let my car go. I guess I'll have to take a cab from your place to mine."

She ran her fingers down the lapels of his jacket and in one quick motion flipped the collar up around his neck. "We'll cross that bridge when we come to it." Then she pulled his face down to hers.

Gerick saw the mischievous glint in her eyes just before their lips met, and he smiled.

Chapter Eight

$\mathcal{A}$yn leaned back on her elbows and stared at the red and gold world of Central Park. It was one of those autumn days that required a sweater and left her cheeks tingling with an exhilarating freshness. She closed her eyes, let her head drop back and listened to the world around her.

In the darkness the blended noises became individual sounds. There was the high-pitched laughter of children playing and the low murmur of a nearby lovers' quarrel. She marveled at how the staccato click of footsteps on the walkway was a direct counterbalance of the labored breaths of the joggers. Now and then an oar slapped the surface of the lake with brilliant clarity. A muted instant later came the swoosh that sprayed droplets to fall like silvery bells on the mirrored surface of the water.

She smiled at the beautiful music of life that was

playing in her ears. A feeling of apprehension overcame her as she thought of the symphony she'd
created. She sat up suddenly and pulled her knees
toward her chest. Wrapping her arms around her
legs, Ayn hugged them close.

"What's wrong?" Gerick asked.

She glanced at the steady rise and fall of his chest.
He was stretched out beside her on the red plaid
blanket, his eyes still closed. "I thought you were
asleep."

"Just thinking."

Not wanting her own thoughts to be questioned,
she didn't ask Gerick what he was thinking about.
He supplied the answer anyway.

"I was imagining how sore I'm going to be tomorrow."

She laughed. "Concert violinists are supposed to
be in great shape."

"Apparently, rowing a boat all over that blasted
lake requires a whole different set of muscles than
playing a concerto."

"I told you that you didn't have to show off for
me."

He opened one eye and squinted to see her
silhouette against the afternoon sun. "That was
not showing off, that was merely getting back to
shore."

"That was showing off."

His laugh was a low rumble. "Well, maybe a
little."

"Roll over," she ordered.

"Gladly."

She moved closer and began massaging his shoulders. "Better?"

"Much. Now, are you going to tell me what's bothering you?"

She hesitated. It had always been hard for her to talk about her problems. "Oh, it's nothing really."

He rippled his back muscles. "Then rub, woman, rub!"

Ayn kneaded the taut cords of his neck vigorously.

"Ouch!" He rolled onto his back and looked at her for a long moment. She met his stare, then finally turned away. Gerick let his fingers walk up the sleeve of her sweater, then slide down to her hand. "I haven't seen that look for quite some time. This tour is getting to you more than you're letting on, isn't it?"

She drew imaginary circles on the blanket. "I'm beginning to think I've failed before I've started."

"Nonsense." He rolled onto his side, resting his head in his hand. "Why you've—"

"Sh-h-h. Listen!"

He obeyed for a moment, then shook his head. "I hear a hundred different things. What am I supposed to hear?"

"Just that. A hundred different sounds make up this small corner of one park in New York. How can I dare to think I've captured the feelings and the sounds of the whole city when one tiny section is so intricate?"

"A composer can't reproduce every variation. What he can do is create a melody broad enough to allow the listeners to hear and see those nuances for themselves."

She sighed. "My mind tells me you're right, but my heart can't help being a little scared." She sat cross-legged. "I want your honest opinion. What do you think of my symphony?"

He rolled·his eyes. "I've told you before."

"No, Gerick. This time I want to hear what you really think. What's your gut feeling about it?"

"I'd give it a seventy-five. It has a nice beat, but it's hard to dance to."

She moaned and fell back. "You're impossible."

"But lovable," he said, pecking her cheek. Standing, Gerick lifted the corner of the blanket and gave it a shake. "Come on. We should be heading home. It'll be dark soon."

Ayn looked at him, confused. The day had been too perfect, too romantic, to let it end so abruptly. She cursed herself for bringing up the subject of her symphony. "Let's not go just yet." She patted the place beside her. "I promise not to talk or to even think about business."

Again he shook the blanket. "Start repacking the hamper and I'll fold this. Then, if you're a real good girl and don't discuss music anymore, I have a surprise for you."

Ayn stood and began gathering the remains of their picnic. She glanced at him. "What's my surprise?"

"I told you last time, it's not a surprise if I tell you."

"I know, I know." She flipped the latch on the basket. "Tell me this: Is it worth being good for?"

He winked. "You'll see."

"That's the most horrible folding job I've ever seen." She moved to stand opposite him. They shook the blanket open, then started over. When Gerick stepped in front of her to bring his half together, they stopped simultaneously. A look passed between them.

"Have I told you how much I love you?" she asked softly.

"Almost as many times as I've told you."

She was serious, and she wanted him to know she was. "I mean it, Gerick. I truly do mean it."

The blue of his eyes glistened with tenderness. "I know, Ayn. I know . . . and I mean it too." The blanket fell to the ground and he gently eased her head to lie against his chest.

The hypnotic beat of his heart lulled her thoughts while he toyed with the satin ribbon in her hair. She threw her arms around his waist. Immediately his left hand was on her lower back drawing her closer and his other arm curled protectively around her shoulders. The embrace seemed to separate them from the world. Gerick's long, slender fingers fanned across her shoulder and upper arm and she bent her head to kiss them.

Ayn wanted them to be so happy, and why shouldn't they be? Gerick's career was set and her career was about to get its biggest chance. Best of all, they were together again. Everything was perfect, wasn't it?

The answer came in the form of a chill dancing down her spine. Although he hadn't said it yet, Ayn knew Gerick's idea of perfect would demand more than she could give. Why couldn't he be satisfied to let things ride? If they could only avoid a confrontation until after the premier of her score, then she would be able to think clearly.

When he spoke her name she sensed it was coming. "Ayn, I don't want to lose you again."

"Nor I you." Her words were muffled against the heavy jersey knit of his shirt.

"I'd give up anything to keep you. *Anything!*"

She looked up suddenly. "No! No, Gerick." Tears filled her eyes and she suddenly felt his hold was suffocating her. With an unexpected strength she broke free from him and moved away.

Gerick caught her wrist and pulled her back to him. Her hands flew up to the solid wall of his chest. His long fingers trapped both her wrists while his other hand circled her waist, imprisoning her against him. "Don't run from me," he commanded in a stern voice.

Run from him was exactly what she did want to do. She wanted to run so she wouldn't have to think about what he'd just said. She'd left him once to keep him from sacrificing his career—or had she left to avoid his asking her to sacrifice? The thought violently robbed Ayn of her last scrap of self-control.

A sob choked past the burning ache in her throat. God, she didn't want it to come to that. It wasn't fair for either of them to have to choose love over career. Yet, music itself was such a passionate, demanding lover that it left little else to give to another.

"Sh-h-h," Gerick soothed. Then he kissed the top of her head. "Hush, Ayn. Don't cry, darling. Please, don't cry."

She looked up into his blue eyes and was seduced by the bewitching fervor in them. Ayn knew what he wanted to hear. Though she didn't believe it, she tried to be as idealistic as he was. Maybe love could conquer all.

"Gerick, I . . . I . . . oh, I can't say it." She looked away and sniffed. "But I love you just as much."

"Of course you do." He hugged her as though he could never get enough of her. "I was wrong to expect you to reciprocate." He placed his hands on either side of her face and gently wiped away her tears. "At least you're honest. Not that what I said wasn't true right now, at this very moment, but I was just letting my heart speak for itself." He sighed. "I know that the minute I'm not looking into your eyes, or holding you, I'll have to admit I was wrong."

"Then hold me," she whispered. "Please, just hold me."

Gerick stroked her hair and stared unseeing across the lawn. She was as scared as he was. He could almost hear Jonathan's warning from the previous night. "Be patient. In time Ayn will give you the commitment you need, but not yet." His lack of restraint filled him with disgust. He hadn't intended to say what he had.

Squaring his shoulders, Gerick forced a laugh. "Hey, look at us. We're acting like the world is ending." He pasted a grin on his face and held her at arm's length. "Why, we have the whole evening still ahead of us, and your surprise."

She gave a quick smile and nodded.

"That will never do," he said, tickling her chin. "I want to see a real smile. Come on, Ayn, smile for me, come on. Oh, oh, I can almost see it. It's coming—aha! There it is."

She laughed; she had to. If he could present a happy facade, so could she. Soon their fake happiness would seep through the masks they wore and they'd temporarily forget the future.

Gerick scooped up the blanket and slung it over his shoulder, then picked up the hamper. "Let's take this thing one day at a time. Okay?"

She agreed and they walked down the Mall. "I must look awful," Ayn said as they weaved through the crowd watching a mime.

Gerick dodged a skater with a large portable radio balanced precariously on his shoulder. Then he studied her. "I don't know, I think puffy eyes and a red nose is quite becoming."

"You're supposed to say I look beautiful all the time and make me feel good."

"You look beautiful all the time and make me feel good."

She jabbed his side. "You're a wise guy . . ." The sentence trailed off when Ayn noticed how protectively Gerick covered his side. "I forgot, you're very ticklish there, aren't you?"

"Absolutely not," he said, his jaw tilted upward. "You must be thinking of one of your other male companions."

She inched toward him, her fingers twitching with mischief. Lunging, her hand brushed him.

When he started he sounded firm. "Ayn!" But his voice ended high with laughter. "Don't."

She continued her fiendish attack, but Gerick managed to sidestep her. Finally she found her target and her fingers feathered up his ribs. The uninhibited laughter that burst from him made Ayn pause. For a brief moment she saw the little boy in Gerick and she loved that side of him too.

He used her lapse in concentration to back away. Snapping from her daze, Ayn confronted him in a standoff. Gerick's face grew serious. "Now cut it out, Ayn." Suddenly his eyes widened and he pointed. "Watch out for that Frisbee!"

Ayn knew the minute she reacted that he'd faked her out, but he was already sprinting toward the car. The top was down on the M.G. and Gerick dropped their things into the space behind the seat. He turned just as Ayn caught up with him. She realized with his hands free she was no adversary. Still, Ayn couldn't resist one last attempt.

"Behave," Gerick warned, easily fending her off. "Remember, I said you only get your surprise if you're a good girl."

She eyed him cautiously. "And just what is my surprise?"

"What did we used to do every Saturday night?"

The memory made her smile. It was so simple, yet so wonderful. "We'd go to Charlie's Chinese Kitchen and splurge."

"One carryout dinner split two ways is hardly a splurge." He grinned. "I get the egg roll."

"Oh, no! I distinctly remember. It's my turn to get the egg roll."

Gerick opened the door for her. "I'll Indian-wrestle you for it."

"You're on."

As they drove down Fifth Avenue, twilight began to ease over the city. The long shadows from the tall buildings made the air feel even cooler. She became aware again of the multitude of sounds that were New York City. Remembering her vow not to even think about her music, Ayn ignored her feelings.

The drive to the hole-in-the-wall restaurant was short. Ayn was amazed that the old couple who owned the place seemed to remember them. Charlie's wife kept giggling and speaking to him in their native tongue as she stacked numerous white boxes into a large sack. Uneasy at their knowing looks, Ayn began to look around. When her gaze fell on the tabloid spread open on the counter, she was horrified.

"Gerick!" Her voice was two octaves above its normal pitch. "Look at this."

He glanced at the headline and the picture of the two of them. With a lift of his eyebrows, he shrugged. "Terribly unflattering. I wish they'd get better photographers."

Charlie bobbed his bald head. "Much better last week."

Ayn gasped. "We were in here last week too?" Her stomach knotted at the thought. She'd hoped after the first mention of them in the gossip column that she could keep their names from being linked.

"Why does it bother you?" Gerick asked, motioning her out the door. "It's good publicity." He waved to Charlie and his family through the street-front window.

Ayn rolled her eyes at his lack of empathy. "You can afford a glittery reputation. You're a man."

Gerick stopped. "Talk about a sexist attitude."

"It's not what I think, it's what they think."

"And just who are *they?*"

"They are the critics and public who are waiting for me or any woman in the field of classical music to do something wrong. Then they can say, 'See, we told you she wasn't serious about music.'"

"Ayn, I know it was hard after San Francisco, when you found out most orchestras only wanted you because they thought it was 'cute' to have a woman conductor, but those days are gone."

"I'm not sure they'll ever be gone."

"When you more or less told those stuffed shirts in Europe that you didn't need them and you came back to America, that's when your status changed. They said, 'Not only is she talented, but she's serious.'"

Talking about her old struggles made Ayn tired and less than diplomatic. "That sounds very sweet, Gerick, but how would you know? You were hopscotching the globe then, winning competition after competition."

"But I knew what was happening with your career every minute. Besides, I was one of those nonbelievers who thought you were a novelty that would fade."

Ayn sat on the hood of Gerick's car and stared sadly at him. "You doubted me too?"

"No, I never doubted you. I always knew you had the talent and even the determination. My reasons for siding with the general consensus were selfish. I hoped you'd have your moment of glory, then realize it was enough and come home to me." He glanced down to the pavement. "Please, Ayn, don't criticize a fool's romantic dreams."

She shook her head. No, she wouldn't criticize him. How could she reprimand someone for loving her? Studying the wings of silver at his temples, she wondered if he looked as beautiful to others as he looked to her. There was no denying his physical attractiveness, but she knew the beauty of his soul and it had to color her perspective of him. For an instant she felt sorry for the rest of the world because they would never know Gerick as she knew him.

Yet, even as Ayn realized how wonderful it was to have a man like Gerick love her, she also realized his love came with conditions. Thoughts swirled inside her, temporarily blinding her. She wasn't even sure if Gerick knew his own conditions, but he soon would. He was going to suggest they move in together again, and when he did, the stipulations would begin to come out. Ayn was so sure about what Gerick wanted. If she could only be as sure about what she wanted.

It took her a moment to associate the waving in front of her eyes with Gerick's hand. "Earth to Ayn, this is earth calling Ayn. Please come in, space cadet."

She laughed at his nonsense. "Sorry. I guess I was a few million miles away. It's just—"

Gerick shook his head, halting her words. "You promised no more business. I'll share the blame this time, but if it happens again I'm afraid it's the firing squad at dawn."

She saluted him, grateful for the reprieve from her gloomy thoughts. "Begging your pardon, sir, but what shall we do till dawn?"

He winked. "I'll think of something. Meanwhile, let's eat before this stuff gets any colder." He started away.

"Where are you going?"

"The rice will get lumpy if we drive all the way back to your apartment."

"Then where would you suggest we go?" Ayn asked, placing her hand on her hip.

He smiled. "My place."

"You mean I finally get to see the best-kept secret in town?"

"Come on," he said, nodding his head toward the intersection. "It's just around the corner."

Ayn wet her lips. She looked at the street sign to reassure herself that Charlie's was still in the same location. It was. She gave Gerick a wry look and wondered if her assumption was possible. Their old apartment had been in the next block. She shook her head; he couldn't still live there.

When she rounded the corner and the brownstone came into view, she stopped. "Oh, Gerick," she said, then bit her bottom lip to keep it from trembling.

He nudged her. "Don't cry, doll. I fixed it up since we lived there."

Like a weary traveler who'd finally seen the lights of home, she felt a sweet sense of relief. A thousand memories filled her mind and she slumped against Gerick. She spoke through hot tears. "You're a sentimental old fool."

"Well, it looks like you're an old softie yourself."

As they reached the outside door, Rosy swung it open. "Glory be, it is you!" The old woman ushered them into the foyer. "I thought I was hallucinating when I looked out the window and saw you two standing on the corner."

"You still live here too?" Ayn asked.

"I keep an eye on things when Mr. Grier is away, and he lets me have the bottom floor at a discount. Too big of a discount, I might add."

Gerick waved off her compliment. "We have enough food here to feed an army. Why don't you come on up?"

Rosy winked a false eyelash at them. "Another time, maybe."

Gerick started up the stairs and Ayn followed. She paused and looked back at Rosy. The old woman was staring at them, her eyes misting as though she were watching a sad late movie on TV.

"Welcome home, Ayn," she said.

Ayn knew she should correct Rosy, but she couldn't. For a moment she wanted to believe that she had stepped back in time and was home again.

Once inside the living area, her eyes saw the renovated spaciousness, but her mind saw the tiny apartment she'd left too many years ago. She was transfixed, afraid if she moved it would all blink away. Her gaze took in the room where they'd laughed and they'd cried. She remembered how hard they'd worked there and how eagerly they'd played.

Gerick seemed unaffected by her presence in the room. He dropped the sack on the coffee table and began to unload its contents. "Why don't you get us some plates?" he suggested. "I'm starved."

Trying to ignore the bittersweet memories that had overcome her, Ayn walked into the kitchen. Having shared so much with Gerick, she knew exactly which cabinet the dishes would be in. When she returned to the living room and glanced at him, she froze. Gerick was standing in front of the window as he had done the last morning they'd been together in the apartment. Her grip loosened and one of the plates slipped from her hand, crashing to the floor.

At the noise, Gerick turned instantly. He was kneeling in front of her almost before she could bend down to retrieve the broken pieces.

"I'm sorry," she kept repeating, hurriedly gathering the bits of earthenware. Their hands met when they reached for the same piece. As though their touch were magnetic, the force pulled their faces up and their eyes locked on each other. A hundred midnights flashed through Ayn's mind. In their bedroom he had followed her down in the darkness and made love to her. She had believed then that no one had ever loved as they had. Surely the communion they shared was not common to everyone. It was special—it had to be. She had always felt their love was sanctioned by something greater than they could ever conceive.

Gerick's large hand cupped her chin and he drew her face to his. His kiss was hesitant at first, a slow tasting of the fullness of her lower lip. When he pulled away and gazed at her, it was a look that was as tantalizing as his kiss had been. He didn't need her consent to continue, but she understood that he wanted it. Ayn gave it willingly.

Gently he took the pottery chips from her and placed them on the floor. Then his strong hands gripped her shoulders and he lifted her to stand. Ayn couldn't control the tremor that shook through her. The need within her was almost desperate in its intensity, and she clung to him. Gerick's left hand slid to her lower back and he pressed her close to him. His hold was protective and comforting, but it was not driven by the same desire as Ayn's.

She closed her eyes and laid her head against his chest. The rhythm of his heart defied the calm exterior he presented. Still, she sensed something was wrong. That same undercurrent that had over-shadowed their happiness the whole day was back. Ayn cursed the fates as she wondered why it had to happen at that moment. There must be something she could do to ease his discontent. The only defense she knew was the one she'd tried all day—recapturing those old feelings. If he'd only waited a little longer they would have made it.

She distanced herself enough to gaze up into his face. The withdrawn look in his eyes made her want to shudder. There was a coldness in his stare that told her he would resist any attempt she made toward intimacy, but she had to try. She'd given up once, accepting his retreat at face value. This time she wouldn't give up without a fight. Their love was worth saving.

"Gerick, love me. Love me like we used to."

He shook his head. "No."

The single word was low, almost unaudible, but she would have known his answer without hearing it. There was a sadness in his eyes that was on-ly matched by the resolute lines of his facial features.

"Gerick, I . . ."

The blue of his eyes blazed. "No!" he said, turning away and crossing the room. At the mantel he stopped. Placing one hand on the shelf as if for support, he looked at her.

"Why have you built a wall between us?" she asked.

"It's my fault. I baited a trap and snared my prey, but I don't have the conviction now to go for the kill."

She sat on the arm of an overstuffed chair. "I don't understand."

"I set this up to happen. The Saturday in the park, like we used to spend together. The Chinese dinner. Coming back here to *our* place. Don't you see? I was trying to make us relive the past. I thought that if you remembered how the good times were . . . well, never mind."

So, they'd both been playing the game. "I know you want to be gallant, but I can't let you take all the blame. I'm as guilty as you are." She caught the tail of her sweater between her thumbs and forefingers and held it out. "Do you know how far I had to dig to find this old pullover? It was your favorite. I never understood why I kept it all those years until this morning." She sighed. "I wanted our outing to be a return to yesteryear just as much as you did."

His eyes twinkled and he snapped his fingers. "That's what's different. The ribbon in your hair . . ."

She nodded. "It's the way I used to wear it."

He sat on the couch. "We're a couple of fools."

"Was I wrong to try and regain the best thing I ever had?"

Gerick looked up. More than anything he wanted to believe that he was the best and most important thing in her life, but it was false hope. Her career, her music were the things that filled that place in her soul. He should make her see it, but his heart wasn't in it. Seeing the sadness in her soft brown eyes made him want to take her in his arms and kiss away her fears.

She looked so vulnerable. Why didn't he take advantage of the moment and trap her in dreams of yesterday? It would be so easy. Gerick wanted to feel the harmony of her body beneath him, but it had to be on his terms.

"It's only wrong, Ayn, if we allow our looking back to blind us from looking forward to our future."

Ayn stiffened. She knew what he said was true. They had to move forward; they couldn't continue to stand still. Yet, the thought of their future was so vague. All her tomorrows were indefinite until after the tour.

Gerick stretched his arm out. With a slow seductive curl of two fingers, he beckoned her to join him. She welcomed the feel of his arm around her when she relaxed beside him.

"For tonight, Ayn, let's forget all we've shared and see if there's anything between us now."

Her fingers played nervously at a button on his shirt. "I'm not sure I can separate the two. Part of the reason I love you now is knowing what you were and how you've become what you are today."

"Forget all that." Gerick lifted her chin and gazed at her. "Love me for the man I'll be tomorrow."

He lowered his head, but Ayn pulled back. She wanted more than a kiss. She wanted a whole night of loving him. All she could think of was keeping it light and teasing him into a loving mood that would last.

Her hand covered his lips. "Sorry, but I don't kiss strangers, sir."

Gerick fell against the back of the couch. "Touché. However, strangers in the night is not exactly what I had in mind."

"And just what did you have in mind?"

"I don't know." He looked away. "I honestly don't know. All I do know is I don't want to fall into the habit of loving each other for old times' sake."

"I guess we play it by ear."

Gerick shrugged. "It seems the logical thing to do."

He was slipping; she had to do something. Ayn stood. "Meanwhile, this food is getting awfully cold. Do you have a microwave?"

Relief washed over him at the change of subject. He wouldn't have to find out if she was capable of giving as much love as he needed. At least not yet. With a deep breath he rose. "No self-respecting bachelor would be without one. Follow me." He scooped up the cartons and headed toward the kitchen.

Ayn lounged against the doorframe and watched his domestic abilities. She had to have another chance to win him back, but how? A thought came to her and she struck a provocative pose. Gerick turned to grab a towel and glanced at her briefly before turning back to the food. Then, he stopped. He looked over his shoulder as though he couldn't believe what he'd seen. With a smile, he turned to face her and leaned against the butcher block table.

He grinned. "What's this?"

Ayn tried unsuccessfully to keep from laughing. She held up her hand to request his indulgence. He crossed his arms over his chest and watched her. Solemn again, she used her sexiest voice. "Hey, sailor. Are you new in town?"

Gerick waved off her silliness and turned back to the Moo Goo Gai Pan. A deep laugh rolled from him and he faced her again. "What the hell. Why not?" He sailed the towel over his shoulder and was in front of her in two long strides. "As a matter of fact," he said, "I am rather new here and I was wondering if you could show me the way to your bedroom?"

She winked. "It'll cost you."

"Name your price." He placed his hands on either side of the doorjamb and leaned over her.

"Breakfast in bed."

He tilted his head as though giving the matter serious consideration. "Okay, lady. You drive a hard bargain, but I'm all yours for the night."

"All night?" She frowned. "In that case you'll have to throw in the first crack at the Sunday crossword puzzle."

"Damn. You're a shrewd businesswoman."

"Take it or leave it."

"I'll take it."

Gerick placed one arm around her waist and the other behind her knees. With an agility that surprised her, he lifted her from the floor as he would a child. He moaned as though she were too heavy and staggered down to his knees and back up. "I'm glad I didn't try this after we'd eaten."

Ayn slapped his shoulder playfully. "What a wimp!"

"A wimp, huh?" They were at the bedroom door and Gerick kicked it open. "How's that for sheer brute force?"

"I'm trembling with awe. Remind me to faint later."

Gerick stopped a few feet from the bed. "You want strength, I'll show you strength." He rocked her back in the cradle of his arms. "One . . ."

"No, Gerick!"

"Two . . ."

"Gerick, you wouldn't! Ger-r-i-c-k!"

"Three!"

With perfect aim he tossed her onto the middle of the bed. Gerick lunged down beside her and his arm clamped over her waist, bringing her to an abrupt halt. Her laughter faded and she looked up at him.

In the dark room, his features were shadowed like a Debussy nocturne. Ayn touched his face, lightly tracing the majestic lines and feeling the sensuous texture. Her predefined notions vanished as she discovered a man she'd thought she'd always known. He continued to stare at her as though by doing so he could bring forth the secrets of her soul. Afraid he would do just that, she gently shoved him onto his back. She had to keep it playful.

With hesitant fingers she unbuttoned his shirt. After each new exposure of flesh, Ayn kissed his hard, muscled chest. She savored the salty taste and marveled that his hot flesh didn't sear her lips. Parting the material, she admired the breadth of his physique. Her hands roamed over the sinewy tendons and she found it hard to believe she was touching a mere man. Awareness of the reined power beneath her palms gave her a feeling of enormous conquest. She sensed his delight at her aggressiveness, but she was unsure how long she could hold back her desire for him. With deliberate pleasure her lips traversed the narrow flatness of his stomach.

Gerick moaned and trapped her wrist within his grip. He pulled her up until she lay half across him, their faces only inches apart. His hands sought the silken softness of her hair and he tugged on the ends of the ribbon. The bow loosened and her mahogany curls tumbled free to shroud them. The feel was heavenly and the sight arousing. He stirred beneath her and Ayn fitted her slender body closer to him.

Hardly able to contain the exquisite sensations, he closed his eyes and breathed deeply. Her presence was almost mystical. The air was filled with her perfume and she seemed to be touching him even where she wasn't. It was as though she'd been perfectly fashioned to complement his body. Even without partaking of the sweetness of her lips, he could taste her. The pendulum of her heart beat wildly against his chest like a metronome out of control. He could feel her everywhere around him. Opening his eyes he allowed every sense to be filled with her and drew his hands down to frame her face.

How could someone so delicate and frail stir such primeval instincts within him? He felt like a wild beast who could only be soothed by the music of her love. Unable to resist the allure of her another minute, Gerick's tongue invited her into the depth of his mouth.

It was obvious she expected a light bantering duel and was surprised when he challenged her for supremacy. For a moment Gerick felt her falter. He was afraid she'd pull away from his almost brutal assault and he'd win by default. Then she surprised him; Ayn accepted the contest. He enjoyed the challenge; then, unable to play the game any longer, Gerick let her taste her moment of near victory before he invoked the strength of his passion for her.

He reversed their positions, rolling on top of her. The fit of her beneath him added fuel to the raging emotions inside Gerick. His kiss was meant to devour. He wanted all of her and was relentless in his pursuit. He knew he was demanding too much of her, but he couldn't contain his hunger. For one insatiable moment he wanted Ayn to depend on him for everything, even her breath.

Just at the instant when they seemed bound to be consumed, Gerick pulled away. He turned away and sat on the edge of the bed. The sound of her ragged breathing filled his ears and he placed his elbows on his knees, then bent his head forward to rest in his hands. It was insane. One person could not possess another person, and yet that's what he wanted to do.

Ayn stirred behind him, but he didn't turn. Her hands glided around his waist and she tugged at the tail of his shirt, which was still tucked into his jeans. With her help he automatically shrugged out of the confines of the heavy knit material. Her hands rubbed across the width of his shoulders, then boldly slid down his chest. Only when she arched against him did he realize she'd removed her sweater and bra. The feel of her small, firm breasts against his back sent a new thrill of desire through him.

It was too late. He was obsessed with her and would have no peace until he claimed her. He resolved he would make her need him as much as he needed her. As he turned, Ayn lay back on the bed. Nude from the waist up, her body was radiant, even in the darkness. She opened her arms to him and he accepted the invitation with a tenderness and reverence. His mouth caressed the soft mound of her breast before his teeth gently bit at the taut peak. At the same time his hand worked its magic on her other breast, tantalizing her with unmetered pleasure.

Enflaming a path across her shoulder and neck, Gerick nibbled his way to the hollow behind her ear. A tingling sensation whirled through her, but she couldn't concentrate on one feeling because his hands were continually roaming her body. As though she were a finely tuned instrument, he played her without mercy. To further his onslaught of passion, Gerick's tongue began to flick wickedly at her ear. Her senses reeled and brightly lit colors danced before her.

His hands were at her denim waistband. He quickly unfastened the snap on her jeans. Slowly, ever so slowly, his large hand inched down her stomach. The zipper parted bit by bit. His palm kneaded her pliant flesh while his fingers found the velvety recess below. His name tore from her with a shudder. With one swift movement he finished removing her clothes. Her whole body writhed with a sublime yearning for Gerick.

She closed her eyes and reveled at the splendor building inside her. When she opened her eyes, the spell was temporarily broken by car lights spilling through the open blinds. The beams raced around the room; then, just as the light darted from the room, she saw Gerick.

He'd shed the remainder of his clothing and stood at the foot of the bed staring down at her. Her breath caught in her throat as she took in the glory of him. As quiet as a pianissimo, she uttered her thoughts aloud. "Avatar."

Gerick threw his head back and laughed. "A god

come to earth? Hardly!" He straddled her. The evidence of his arousal caused her to shiver with anticipation. "A god would not think what I'm thinking about you right now."

He superimposed his length on top of Ayn, crushing her deeper into the soft folds of the bed. As he kissed her she knew she was his to do with as he pleased.

She had not prepared for the fierceness of his need. One movement flowed into the next without pause, driven by a single theme. The panorama before her exploded as their rhythmic pulses took them through the impalpable passage just this side of silence.

Gerick was with her at the brink. The chasm below seemed dark, brooding and tortuous. She was afraid to let go, but Gerick arched her toward infinity, defying gravity. They touched the top note like a rising arpeggio soft, sweet and perfect.

Gently, with a thousand caresses, he brought her back. As they descended with a diminuendo grace, Ayn felt she could no longer breathe. She wanted to speak, but her love was too strong for words. All she could do was cling to him desperately. She didn't want the melody of their souls broken. He understood and remained a part of her.

"Ayn," he whispered. "My *raison d'être.*"

His reason for being. She smiled and closed her eyes.

"Come on," Ayn said, one foot on the stoop, the other propping the door open.

Gerick walked down the stairs from his apartment. He held the magazine section of the Sunday paper in front of his face. A pencil was poised above it as if waiting for inspiration. "What's a six-letter word that means to go slow?" he asked absently.

Ayn threw her arms up and went back inside. Grabbing his coat sleeve, she dragged him forward. "G-E-R-I-C-K," she answered.

"Cute, Ayn. Very cute."

She snatched the paper from him and deposited it in the umbrella stand as they left. Linking her arm through his, she pulled him quickly down the stoop. Caught off guard, Gerick had to take the steps two at a time.

"What's the hurry? Washington Square isn't going anywhere."

"I want to get there before all the tourists and crowds."

"Ayn, I'm telling you, Sunday mornings in the Village are not like they used to be. The days of someone like Dylan, or Simon, or Yarrow coming down for an impromptu are gone."

"I know, but it used to be such a special place for us."

"Ayn . . ."

"Don't worry, I'm not slipping back into the past." She reached up and kissed his cheek. "I just feel so wonderful this morning that I couldn't stay inside."

She leaned her head against his shoulder and they walked on, content with the new memories they'd made the night before. Ayn had found new meaning in their relationship that went far beyond the physical. Once again she felt they had discovered that spiritual realm, except it was even better than they'd shared before. Gerick still had some old ideas about their love, but she was sure they had the patience now to endure a period of change and adjustment.

When they reached Washington Square, it was alive with people. Several musicians were setting up under the arch and their instrument cases were laid open, ready for contributions. Gerick guided Ayn to a secluded bench. They sat in silence, holding hands and watching the people in the center of the park.

He spoke her name so softly that she wasn't sure he'd said it. When she looked at him, she knew he had.

"I've been giving this a lot of thought. I know there will be problems to work out, but I'm going to ask you anyway. . . ."

Ayn was surprised at her own excitement. Yes, she wanted to say right then. Yes, I'll live with you. I need you and I love you. She wanted to hear him say the words aloud.

"Ayn, will you marry me?"

Her answer died with her sudden intake of breath. Her mind reeled with the new idea. Marriage! She hadn't even considered that as a possibility. She had assumed they would live together as they had before. In time marriage might work into their lives, but certainly not immediately. Gerick would expect to own her if they married right away.

It was her own stupidity. She should have realized the only reason they hadn't married before was Gerick's lack of money. Income was no longer a problem for him. He could give her all the things he used to dream of giving her. She had been reliving the past and it had blinded her to the future, just as he'd said it would.

The blatant hope shining in Gerick's eyes was too

much for Ayn. She turned away. He was waiting. She needed to say something. All she could think to do was to repeat his question. "Marry you?" She sounded more astonished than she had intended.

He bristled. "Yes, you know, when two people promise to love, honor and cherish each other for as long as they both shall live. You have heard of people doing that, haven't you?"

She'd hurt him, but what made her flinch was his retaliation. Why was love filled with so much pain? "Gerick, I—"

"There's no need to explain. I understand. You just don't love me."

"Stop it, Gerick! I do love you, but I need a few minutes to collect myself. Like you said, there are a lot of things we have to work out." She groped for something to say to stall for time. "I mean, where will we live?"

"My place, of course."

His place, of course. Didn't he realize she had a choice in the matter? "But my apartment is better situated. We'll be gone most of the time, but when we're home, it's closer to everything."

"This is not a business merger we're discussing here. We'll work out the details later."

No, she thought, we must agree now. The details were important, especially the one detail he wouldn't admit even to himself. Before she could marry him, she had to be positive they wanted the same things. "Oh, Gerick. There's just so much being thrown at me all at once."

"There shouldn't be. Haven't you known it would come to this from that first day at the Metronome?"

"No, I didn't think it would come to marriage. I

thought we'd live together awhile and then, well, you know, we'd see how it went and then decide if we wanted to get married or not."

"Living together is not enough for me this time. I want all of you."

Ayn stood and nervously walked back and forth in front of him. "It scares me when you say *all*. I'm afraid that's more than I have to give."

"We both may have to give up certain things in our lives, but won't it be worth it if we have each other?" He trapped her hands between his and stopped her pacing.

Ayn sighed. "Gerick, are you ready to give up your concert tours?"

"No!" he said, indignant.

"Neither am I."

"Is that what you think my proposal means? You think I'm asking you to give up your career?"

"No, you'd never ask me to give it up, but you do expect me to, in time. Just like you expected me to come back to you all those years. As long as you think that way, I'll only end up disappointing you again."

He didn't respond and Ayn knew she was right. She wished she had been wrong. "What you want is someone who's content to be Mrs. Gerick Grier. Someone who will be there to wish you luck when you go on stage and greet you when you come off."

"True. That's the kind of woman I've always dreamed of. Like I said, there will be problems, but we'll adjust. Eventually—"

"No, not eventually, Gerick, never. I won't be there when you come off the stage. I'll either be on the stage with you, or more than likely, I'll be somewhere halfway around the world on a different stage." She knelt in front of him. "Gerick, I'm not the type of someone you want me to be."

He looked at her, defeat in his eyes. "No, I guess you can't be that type of woman, can you?"

Ayn shook her head, sorry she'd had to destroy all his hope. It was necessary, though; she had to make him see the truth. He had to be honest with himself about his expectations or they'd have no chance of making it. The problem was, since she'd taken away all his romantic notions, would he still want her?

"Can you accept me as I am, for who I am, and still be happy with me for the rest of your life?" *Say yes, Gerick, and I'm yours forever. Dear God, make him say yes.*

He hung his head. "I don't know. I just don't know right now."

She stood. "But you do know. Admit it, Gerick. You don't love me for me; you love me for what you want me to be."

"I suppose I do," he said sadly. He released her hands and looked up. Then anger flashed in his lightning blue eyes. "There, I've said it. Are you happy now? Wouldn't a simple no from you have been sufficient?"

"No," she whispered, and turned to walk up Fifth Avenue.

Would no have been enough? Not for Gerick. He wouldn't have let it die until he knew why she couldn't trust their love to blind faith. She did the only thing she could do to keep them from feeling smothered by one another. His disapproval of her career would have been unspoken, but constant. They would slowly end up hating each other.

The numbness began to leave and tears formed in her eyes. If he'd only hinted sooner that all this was inside him. The first clue she'd had was the day before. It had shocked her when he'd said he'd always expected her to give up and come home to him. It had also opened her eyes to a problem she knew he refused to see. Even then, she thought they could handle it in time. Gerick's proposal made it too eminently important. Things Ayn could throw to the fates in a relationship, she couldn't in a marriage. That kind of union was too permanent. Like Gerick had said, it was a for-as-long-as-you-both-shall-live situation.

A shiver rippled through her and Ayn realized she'd walked further than she'd intended. She stopped at the corner and spotted an empty taxi waiting at the traffic light. Signaling him, she let her gaze travel a few blocks back. Gerick was leaning against the arch. It was over. From that point on he was a violinist and she was a conductor.

"Good-bye, Gerick," she said silently. "See you in Moscow."

As she stepped into the cab, Ayn felt completely alone. She gave the driver her address, then she added, "And would you mind turning on a little music? I need some company."

"Sure thing," he said, flipping a knob. "You like music, huh?"

She glanced back at Gerick and wiped away her last tear. Then she turned around. "Music is my life."

Chapter Nine

It took Ayn a moment to realize the plane had broken through the clouds, because when she looked down, a frozen world of forests, fields and wooden villages greeted her. Snow covered everything. Occasionally the green tips of tall pines, their branches flocked and drooping toward the earth, splintered through the cold drifts. In the distance, ashen smoke curled from the chimneys on a row of log cabins barely visible beneath their burden of snow. Otherwise, nothing peeked from under the heavy blanket of white.

Ayn strained against her seat belt trying to see better. Always anticipating her, Jonathan patted her arm.

"Relax, Ayn, you can't see Moscow before we land. No circling patterns are allowed over the city."

She eased back against the seat, enjoying the

tingling excitement building inside her. As technology fought nature for control of the vessel, the powerful engines reversed, causing vibrations to shiver through Ayn. She placed her fingers over her lips to keep from laughing with joy.

Jonathan laughed for her. "I felt the same way when I first came here. Go ahead; let it out. Everyone on this plane should feel the same. To a musician, Russia is thrilling and romantic."

"I still can't believe I'm here. The land that inspired Prokofiev, Stravinsky and Rimsky-Korsakov. Not to mention the grand master, Tchaikovsky."

"And we mustn't forget Rachmaninoff," Jonathan said, leaning closer.

As the wheels of the jet touched the runway, Ayn's mood touched a sad low. Rachmaninoff, she thought, remembering how Gerick had looked at her when he'd played the Paganini Rhapsody that day in September. She glanced a few rows ahead where Gerick sat in rapt conversation with Hank. He hadn't spoken to her for the entire nine-hour flight.

It wasn't until Gerick's broad shoulders filled the aisle that she realized they'd stopped moving and everyone was preparing to disembark. She unfastened her seat belt and began to collect her things.

"I know it's none of my business," Jonathan said, adjusting his flight bag on his shoulder, "but your reaction to the name Rachmaninoff confirmed my suspicions. The weekend didn't go well, did it?"

Ayn fought the irritation rising inside her. Lately, it seemed everyone knew all the intimate details of her life. "You're right," she said, squeezing past him into the main aisle. "It's none of your business."

Jonathan trailed after her. "I tried to tell him recapturing the past won't cure the problems of today."

She continued toward the exit as she looked back over her shoulder. "I'm sick and tired of my personal life being common knowledge to everyone." She turned back just in time to notice the flow of people had stopped. Before she could stop she ran into the solid wall of Gerick's back. Regaining her balance, she straightened and offered a hurried apology. Gerick didn't turn or acknowledge her.

Torn between humiliation and a strong desire to drop her carry-on luggage and throw her arms around him, she closed her eyes. Hot tears stung in the darkness of her thoughts. It should be the happiest day of her life, yet every time Gerick came to mind, nothing else mattered. Opening her eyes, she saw him step to the side. He motioned to the accordion arm leading into Sheremetyevo Airport. The tunnel was almost empty of people now, and Gerick bowed with exaggerated movements.

"Please, go ahead of me, since you seem to be in such a hurry."

Rather than prolong the agony of being near him, she marched past Gerick without speaking.

His voice followed her determined steps. "You're welcome!"

Jonathan caught up with her at the customs counter. She offered her passport and health certificate to the inspector before turning to face him. "Don't say it, Jonathan."

"But Ayn, I hate to see you wasting your life like this."

The stout-looking inspector motioned Ayn to the

next man. "Please," the new inspector said, handing her a form, "declare your money and jewelry." She filled in the appropriate blanks before turning an angry stare on Jonathan.

"Wasting my life, huh? I'm not quite thirty, I've won every major award in my field, and I'm in Russia to conduct at the Grand Hall of the Tchaikovsky Conservatory of Music." She turned suddenly on the inspector. "A real wasted life, wouldn't you say?"

The man looked puzzled. He stamped her form, handed it to her and nodded. "Welcome to Moscow."

"*Spasibo*—thank you," she said, offering the only Russian she felt familiar enough with to use.

Jonathan snatched his declaration form from the inspector and shook it in Ayn's face. "I'm not talking about your career. I'm talking about that 'private life' you want to keep a secret. Well, first you'd better have something worth keeping secret." She started to interrupt, but Jonathan shook his head and continued. "Tell me, Ayn, will your baton go walking with you in Red Square tonight? Or when you've grown old, will your sheet music keep you warm?"

His words didn't surprise her. Ayn had asked herself the same questions. What did hurt was the tone he'd used. Just as she opened her mouth to answer, Gerick stepped up to the counter behind Jonathan. "Forget it," she said, turning and walking away.

"*Kakoy durak!*" Jonathan called after her.

Ayn stopped. "Damn." She juggled her hand luggage and pulled a pocket dictionary from her purse. Thumbing through the pages, she wished she'd listened to her professor and studied Russian. Jonathan breezed by her, repeating the words in a taunting cadence. Ayn rolled her eyes, then continued her search. She found the meaning just as Gerick walked past her offering the translation.

"What a fool!"

"Thanks," she snapped, slamming the book shut.

"Any time," he answered, a low chuckle following his words.

Ayn watched him flip up the collar of his top coat as he walked away. She wanted to hate him, to totally despise everything about him, but she couldn't. At times she could manufacture a mild dislike, but even that faded the instant she saw him again.

She didn't notice the production manager had walked by until he stopped and turned to face her. "You look lost."

She came to life, wondering if he had noticed she was staring at Gerick. "As a matter of fact," she said, groping for something to say, "I am. Where do I pick up my luggage?"

Drawing his brows together, he gave her a strange smile. "Ayn, I'll take care of it like I always do. The bags will be at the hotel and the instruments will be at the concert hall, as usual. Are you sure everything is all right?"

"Yes, I'm fine. Really. Just a case of jet lag, I guess." She hurried down the corridor. "See you later."

Ayn expected cold when she stepped outside, but nothing could prepare her for the cold of Moscow. Her bare hands tingled as though they might crack from the exposure, and the icy air caught in her lungs, creating a cloud of condensation when she exhaled. Jonathan waved his hand to catch her eye and motioned her to join him at a taxi near the curb.

Her smile faded when Gerick stepped up to the small car. A short, rotund man who resembled a bear in his fur coat and matching hat puffed along at Gerick's side.

"Excuse me," Ayn said, starting to leave. "I didn't know this was your cab."

"It's *our* cab," Gerick announced, stopping her retreat. "May I introduce you? Ayn Remington, this is our Intourist agent, Nikolay Zinoviev. Mr. Zinoviev, Ms. Remington."

Ayn shifted her bags and automatically offered her hand to the man. In the best European manner, he took her fingers and delicately placed a kiss on the back of her hand.

"It is an honor, indeed," he said, a reverence in his voice. Then suddenly he straightened and shouted something to the taxi driver. The dark-haired man moved around the car and took her carry-on luggage, then disappeared behind the cab.

"*Spasibo,*" she offered hesitantly.

"Please, Miss Remington, my English is much better than your Russian."

She nodded her agreement as Gerick's voice rose in volume. They turned to see Gerick and the driver in a standoff at the rear of the car. The agent rushed to intercede.

Ayn watched the exchange of strange-sounding words, then turned to her old friend leaning against the sedan. "Jonathan, what on earth is going on?"

"The driver wants Gerick to put his violin in the

trunk, and of course that will only happen over Gerick's dead body."

Nikolay closed the lid with a final burst of Russian to the driver. Gerick smiled triumphantly and tapped the leather of his case possessively.

"Forgive, please," Nikolay said with a shrug. "Our drivers must be able to take apart and put back together an entire car to get their permit, but alas, protocol? Perhaps it is not stressed so much."

Jonathan opened the car door he had been leaning on. His voice was low when he offered Ayn an explanation. "It is not considered cultured to allow any type of baggage in the front of the car. Apparently, a violin case is an exception to the rule—or Gerick is, I'm not sure which."

Ayn laughed as she slid onto the back seat. Gerick's tall body did not fold down so easily when he climbed in. Jonathan saluted them and started to close the door.

"Wait!" Ayn said, leaning across Gerick and looking up at Jonathan. "Aren't you coming with us?"

"No, this sedan is way too little. Three in the back seat? Now *that* would be uncultured."

Nikolay seemed to be fighting with his bulky coat as he took his place in the front next to the driver. "Is true," he said, glancing back at Ayn. "Mr. Eichman has his own Intourist agent."

Ayn fell back against the seat with a heavy sigh. Jonathan closed the door, waved and they sped away. She realized instantly that the back seat was far too small for three people; it even felt too small for two when one of them was Gerick. He had been unusually quiet during her exchange with Jonathan, and though she didn't want to have to cope with being so near him, it hurt to think he was ignoring her. She missed her best friend. She leaned close enough for only Gerick to hear. "Why didn't you explain that we aren't traveling together?"

Still not looking at her, he answered in a whispered voice. "Believe me, this was *not* my idea. The Ministry of Culture thought the two stars should be kept together."

"Something is wrong?" Nikolay asked, turning around.

Gerick motioned to a neon sign they were passing. "Ayn doesn't know the Cyrillic alphabet."

Nikolay's smile was boyish. "Happy Journey Through the USSR."

Ayn nodded her acknowledgment. She slid as far away from Gerick as possible, then folded her arms across her chest and rested against the door. An uneasiness hung in the close space of the car like a thundercloud waiting to unleash its anger.

The driver jerked his head toward the back seat and said something to Nikolay. The agent's face grew red with embarrassment but he laughed.

"Da," Gerick said.

"Yes, what? What did he say?" Ayn asked, irritated at herself for not making the time to learn the language better.

"The driver said it was colder in this back seat than it is outside. He said only a lovers' quarrel brings such hostility. Apparently, New York cabdrivers don't have the monopoly on making unsolicited comments to their passengers."

Ayn didn't find the same humor in the situation that Gerick did. "Listen, why don't we issue a press release every morning? Just in case there's someone out there who doesn't know what's happening in our relationship."

"Do I detect a note of sarcasm in your voice?"

She hated it when he was being charming while she was trying to make a serious point. He knew exactly how to melt her frosty exterior, but she refused to let him know he'd succeeded. "You detect a note of total disgust."

Before he could answer, the car swerved sharply to the right, throwing Ayn against Gerick. The violin case, which had been resting on his knees, fell to the floor, and Gerick's arms circled Ayn protectively as they pulled onto the shoulder.

"What in the . . ." He stopped, seeing the long black limousines speeding past them. The driver removed his cap and Nikolay sat at attention. Ayn and Gerick instantly leaned forward, hoping to recognize one of the dark, bulky forms through the curtained windows.

Their car waited in silence for seconds after the limousines had disappeared around a bend in the road. Gerick finally asked the obvious. "Members of the Party's Presidium?"

"Perhaps," Nikolay said, motioning the driver back onto the road.

Gerick smiled at the evasive answer and said something to Nikolay in his own language. The agent grinned, and then they returned to English and fell into an easy conversation about Gerick's previous visit to the Soviet Union.

Ayn stared out the window at the endless white stretching to the horizon. Suddenly a heavy horse-drawn sled hurried across the snow. The occupants of the sled were wrapped in so many layers for warmth that it looked as though they might roll off the slab seat at any moment. Their destination came into view: a line of tiny wooden houses. The structures were decorated with bright paint on the ornate doors and window frames, causing them to look like dollhouses.

"It looks like a fairy-tale town," she said, more to herself than to anyone else.

"Pre-Revolutionary." Nikolay stated the fact without inflection in his voice. Then the agent turned back to Gerick and they continued comparing the changes in the area from the last time Gerick had toured there.

Ayn turned away from the two men. The open fields began to give way to the suburbs. Apartment buildings, ten and twelve stories high, stood between massive groves of pine and birch trees.

"This is the new *Mockba*," Nikolay said, using the Russian pronunciation of the city name. "In the past seven years over six hundred thousand new flats have been completed and occupied."

"Very nice. I can see why you're proud of the new Moscow."

Her simple statement brought a warmth to Nikolay's watery gray eyes. He explained that apartment complexes were not allowed inside Moscow Ring Road, only in the outskirts such as these in the Forest-Park Protection Belt. "The center of our city must be preserved as it is, for the future generations."

By the time they entered the city limits, the atmosphere inside the cab had relaxed. Everyone was friendly and conversation flowed freely. As

Nikolay and Gerick pointed out numerous sights, a realization finally eased over Ayn. This was a country that was vastly different from any other place she'd ever seen.

People were everywhere. Their cumbersome shapes, bundled against the cold, hurried along as though driven by the snow. Every so often there were glass-cased reading boards where dozens of men with fur caps pulled low over their ears stood reading the latest edition of *Pravda*. The crowds seemed conscious of the freezing temperature, but not bothered by it. At least once in each block there was a woman with a broom sweeping the snow from the sidewalks. Woolen scarves pulled tight and framing their round, red faces made them each look like a clone of the other.

On several corners were brightly colored little stalls. "Kiosks," Nikolay offered. "They sell cigarettes, theater tickets and food. The usual snacks, cakes, fruit pies and flavored drinks. Oh, yes, they also have—"

"Ice cream?" Ayn asked, suddenly seeing a man bite into a chocolate-covered pop.

"Yes," Nikolay said, his face beaming with delight. "We Muscovites are tough."

Ayn shivered at the thought; then it happened. Without warning, Gerick took her hand in his. Heat radiated through her and she felt as though life had suddenly been breathed into her lifeless form. Alive again, her senses tingled with an electric anticipation and she looked up into Gerick's eyes. The instant that his gaze caught hers, Ayn knew her feelings hadn't changed. She still needed, she still wanted Gerick for the rest of her life.

It was only when the world seemed right that she realized what had been wrong. Though it had been less than two days since she'd looked into the liquid blue of his eyes, it felt as though she'd been without him for an eternity.

How on earth was she going to finish the season with Gerick? When they'd tried to stay apart before, at least they'd been friends and there'd been hope. The hope had died. Even the memories were painful. There was no solace in remembering.

Seeing him look at her as he did, Any wanted to melt into his arms and promise him anything. Perhaps she could give up the conducting. Andrews wanted her to write another Broadway musical. Then she could travel with Gerick. It had been a fun challenge before. Maybe it would be enough again. Who was she kidding? Only herself; she was born to conduct.

Gerick pointed across a street three times wider than Park Avenue. It took a few seconds for her to focus on the corner building. At first she saw only the Greek Revival architecture, the grooved columns topped with scrolled capitals; then she gasped.

"The Tchaikovsky Conservatory," she whispered. "Oh, Gerick, I can't believe it."

"It's yours, Ayn," he said, squeezing her hand. "I think it was Napoleon who said, 'If I capture Moscow then I have taken Russia by her heart.' Go for the heart, Ayn."

In the shadow of the great hall, Ayn felt a moment of doubt. "Do you think I can?"

"I know you can," Gerick said, as the light changed and they continued down Gorky Street.

Ayn glanced back over her shoulder, then at

Gerick. He had meant it, he truly believed she could do it. Was he learning to accept her career? No, she thought sadly, he'd always encouraged and supported her. If they couldn't make each other happy, he wanted her to have the happiness of music.

"Did you know that Tchaikovsky was the first to conduct at Carnegie Hall when it opened?" Nikolay asked, drawing her thoughts back inside the car.

When the cab pulled up to a stop, they hadn't finished their discussion of how the arts break down the political boundaries of the world. Ayn frowned when she saw the rather shabby-looking hotel.

"It's equivalent to the St. Regis," Gerick said, as Nikolay and the driver jumped from their seats to open the back doors for their guests. Ayn glanced at the narrow door under a portico shaped like a piano lid and forced a smile for the driver. Gerick and Nikolay joined her and Gerick took her by the shoulders and turned Ayn around to face the street.

"My God," she said, pointing to a tall brick wall. "We're across from the Kremlin."

"All visitors should see the seat of Soviet power." Nikolay pointed across Manege Square. "There, at the far end of Red Square, is Rossiya Hotel. You must dine at the restaurant on the twenty-first story of the tower wing. A most magnificent view of the Kremlin and the square." They turned back to face their own hotel and Nikolay winked. "The National, inside, has a wonderfully romantic old-style atmosphere. Is good, yes?"

Gerick offered his arm to escort Ayn. "Yes, Nikolay, it is good."

All the romantic atmosphere in the world couldn't help them, but Ayn took his arm. What marvelous actors they were. Inside, the lobby was elegant with high ceilings, but Ayn was amazed at how small it was. There was a newsstand at one end and the registration desk was located at the other end; in between there were three hard, straight-backed chairs.

While Nikolay checked them in, Ayn sat on one of the chairs and drew in a long breath. She told herself that traveling for such an extended period had made her tired. Yet she knew the real reason for her sudden drained feeling was the roller-coaster ride her emotions were taking. It was thrilling to be in Russia, but Gerick haunted her every minute. Just the thought of him made her feel depressed.

When Nikolay returned, he spoke to Gerick in Russian. They shook hands, and he patted Gerick's back as though they were old friends. With a polite nod to Ayn, the agent left. Gerick took Ayn's elbow and lifted her to her feet without a word. He led her around the corner where two elevators faced each other. The elevators opened beneath white plaster arches and the arches were supported by nude statues of male athletes. A small man in a worn brown uniform greeted them, then closed the scrolled brass door. They only rode one floor.

"The V.I.P. floor," Gerick said as they stepped out.

Ayn haulted abruptly when she saw a stout-looking woman sitting squatly between the elevators. The woman perused them up and down, then offered her question.

"Room number?"

Gerick gave the woman the numbers and she

handed him two keys. Ayn stared in amazement until Gerick gently pulled her away.

"Hall monitor?" she joked.

"Exactly. Though they're called floor matrons."

"You're kidding."

Gerick slipped the key into the lock of Ayn's room. "I'm totally serious." He dropped the key in her hand. "You'll need to give this to her every time you leave and pick it up when you return."

Ayn looked back at the woman, who flashed her a silver-toothed grin. "Who am I to argue? When in Moscow, do as the Muscovites do, but I'm not going to eat ice cream when it's snowing."

Gerick laughed; then, looking down at her hand, he gently closed her fingers over the key. His hand remained to cover hers and they looked into each other's eyes. Ayn was afraid to breathe, afraid the moment would pass. Slowly the magic faded and he offered her a sad smile. She heard his unspoken words in her mind. It's over.

"There you are," Jonathan's voice came at them from down the hall. "You won't believe this, but Lenin stayed in my room. In fact he gave speeches from my balcony." He stopped, seeing their intimate looks. "I think I'm interrupting something." Jonathan turned around and headed back to his room.

"No," Gerick called, breaking the spell of their gaze. "I was just leaving."

Ayn forced herself to look at Jonathan. If Gerick could pretend nothing had happened, so could she. "Come back here," she said, opening the door to her room.

Jonathan stood between the now-curious floor

matron and Ayn's room. He shrugged. "I just wanted to tell both of you that the whole orchestra is planning to meet in the hotel restaurant in about thirty minutes. We thought it would be fun to dine together. Besides, someone has to translate the ingredients of this rich food."

"Thank you," Gerick said, "but I'll be dining in my room." He nodded to each of them, then strolled away.

Ayn wondered if she looked as shocked as Jonathan did as she watched Gerick enter his room. Setting her personal turmoil aside, she thanked Jonathan and added, "If my luggage arrives in time, I'll change and meet you for dinner."

Jonathan glanced at Gerick's room and then closed the distance between himself and Ayn. "Is everything all right? I mean with you and Gerick?" he asked in a hushed tone.

She tried to lie convincingly. "Everything's fine."

"Well, if you're sure." He backed away a few steps.

"I'm sure, Jonathan."

"I know my official capacity on this trip is advisor for the orchestra, but I'm pretty good at advice to the lovelorn, too."

"I'll remember that. Thanks for caring."

Alone in her room, Ayn wanted to fling herself across the bed and cry, but she couldn't allow that kind of release. If she did, she might not stop, and she had a hundred and twenty-five people depending on her. Ayn couldn't translate for them as Jonathan could, but as conductor she was needed in an entirely different role. Ayn was their symbol of strength and unity. As strangers in a strange land, they needed to see her exuding her authority at least over them. The average age of the musicians in ISO was much younger than the members of other, more established orchestras. Because of that fact, very few of them had ever toured overseas, and none had been to Russia before. Jonathan used to refer to the orchestra as his children, and Ayn was finding that her maternal instincts were growing stronger each day. She sighed. There was no time to cry for a love that could never be. ISO was the only family she'd ever have and they needed her right then.

Gerick sat staring out of his hotel window. Evening had settled over Moscow like a soft silver blanket. His thoughts were not serene. They were swirling, caught in the vortex of too many conflicting emotions. Until that morning at Washington Square, not once had he consciously realized that if Ayn followed him around as he had dreamed of her doing, she'd have to give up conducting. What a fool he was not to have seen it earlier. Yet, even with the chance of losing her forever, he doubted he could change his feelings.

All his life he'd dreamed of one person to love him more than anything and anyone. Even his own mother had not understood his career in great music. She died wanting him to settle down and get a normal job with a regular orchestra. Gerick had never been sure if she'd wanted it because she thought playing in a local philharmonic was secure or if she never really believed his talent as a virtuoso was good enough and would last. He had no other family and had not taken the time to develop close friendships, except with Ayn.

With all he'd gained over the years, he'd remained just a man going through the motions of living until she was back in his life. Gerick the carefree, happy-go-lucky guy with millions of adoring fans and hundreds of swooning women at his feet was just a facade of a lonely boy who'd grown into a lonely man.

Though he believed in his own abilities, he still needed the physical presence of that one special person who also believed in him. Ayn was that person. He wanted her with him every minute of every day. The thought of settling for less of her seemed ludicrous and impossible. If he didn't accept her terms, though, he'd have none other.

He kept trying to rationalize. She wasn't asking so much. It was quite reasonable and some men would give in. He'd heard of long-distance marriages and many seemed to work out fine, but they couldn't be assured of every weekend. He might go months without seeing her. That was no kind of a marriage, not for Gerick. He couldn't live that way. Maybe after the success of her . . . maybe, maybe, maybe. He was grabbing at any loose straw he could find, but the answer always came out the same.

If he was a man, a real man, he'd sever the ties. They both needed to be free so they could start rebuilding their lives again. As long as they were together, seeing each other and being close, they'd cling to those old memories. The shock of finally knowing what he must do sat him bolt upright in his chair.

Slowly he went to the phone. After quite a delay he was talking with his agent in New York. "I don't care how it will look," Gerick said, drawing his hand down over his face. "This is the way I want it. It's the only choice I have. . . . I don't give a damn what you have to do about the contracts, just do it. And Bill, not a word of this goes to the press until after the concert." He swallowed. "I owe her that much, at least."

Returning the receiver to its cradle, he waited for the flood of relief that he expected. It didn't come and he worried if he'd made the right decision. He shook his head. Right or wrong he was going to see it through. With mechanical motions he resumed his vigil at the window.

How many times had he seen the hourly change of guards at Lenin's tomb? Three maybe four times, he'd lost track, but somehow the punctual regard for their country's honored dead had linked him to reality. Normally Gerick was a level-headed man, but when it came to Ayn he'd only thought among the clouds of his dreams. For once he'd touched the ground.

Then he noticed the figure crossing Marx Prospect. The hood of the white fur coat was pulled up around her face, but he knew her walk, even from the distance. It was Ayn, but what was she doing out? Since the sun had left the sky hours ago, the temperature must have dropped bitterly. She's probably going walking in Red Square, he thought, a rueful smile on his lips. He should be with her, but he'd made a decision and he had to stick with it, for both their sakes.

Suddenly Ayn turned around and went back to the curb. Gerick couldn't believe his eyes when she hailed a taxi. Since he couldn't get to her in time to stop her, the only hope was that the driver didn't speak English—but so many of them did. "Damn!" he said, slapping the arm of the chair as she stepped into the cab and drove off. In a flash, Gerick grabbed his coat from the wardrobe closet and dashed for the door.

Starting for the elevators, Gerick stopped when he had another thought. He hurried to Jonathan's room. His knocks on the frosted glass top of the door were persistently anxious.

"Yes, yes, I'm coming," Jonathan called. "Hold your horses." He opened the door. "Oh, hello Gerick, come in."

"Do you know where Ayn was going?"

"Going? Why, no, I left her at her room. She didn't mention going anywhere."

"I just saw her get into a cab and head down Gorky Street."

"Well, they say it's quite safe to travel around Moscow at night. Very little crime here, you know. I suppose—" Jonathan gasped when he finally realized what Gerick was concerned about. "You say she took a cab going away from the center of the city?"

Gerick nodded.

"Oh, dear, doesn't she know they won't pick up single women and bring them back in? Especially an American woman. It does seem silly, I mean you'd think—"

"Jonathan," Gerick interrupted. "Where would she have gone? I need to go after her."

"Well, let me see. She doesn't know a soul here." He tapped his jaw. "Gorky Street, huh? There's the Aragvi, a great Georgian restaurant. They have a *kharcho* that's just this side of heaven—"

"Jonathan! She just had dinner with you, didn't she? Now, where would Ayn have gone?" Gerick snapped his fingers just as Jonathan came up with the same answer. "The conservatory," they said in unison. "Thanks," Gerick called, already heading off.

Only when the driver stopped in front of the conservatory was Ayn sure he'd understood her one-word command of "Tchaikovsky." She pulled a bill out and offered him a questioning look. He nodded it was enough, then handed her back some coins, but Ayn waved them away. He grinned broadly enough to let her know she'd made him a very happy man.

As she walked up to the entrance of the great hall, Ayn doubted her reasoning for the first time since she'd decided to make the journey. She knew it would probably be closed, but she needed to think and an empty concert hall was the best place for her. To Ayn's surprise the massive door opened with great ease for its height.

Reverence filled her as she stepped into the partially lit building. It was a feeling even greater than she'd experienced at Carnegie Hall. There was something almost magical about the grand old halls that inspired awe in her. She removed her coat and placed it on a chair in the back row. Slowly, Ayn walked down the aisle, moving as though the ground were hallowed and must not be bruised by her steps.

She turned a complete circle to try to take in the total beauty of the massive room. Eight huge crystal chandeliers were suspended from the ornate ceiling.

There were intricately carved columns that extended floor to ceiling supporting the side boxes that looked down from a second level. Her wonder was interrupted by a burst of strange-sounding words.

Ayn whirled around, easily able to tell where the voice came from in this room with perfect acoustics. A rather ominous-looking man stepped from the shadows of the stage entrance. Before Ayn realized she needed to respond to him, he boomed again at her.

"I'm sorry. I don't speak Russian. I'm American."

He moved toward her. "American?" he said as though the word hurt him to speak it.

Ayn decided to meet him partway, but he pointed a finger at her and spoke in a wild tone that indicated she should stay where she was. As he covered the distance between them, Ayn focused on his clothes and on the set of jangling keys on his belt. He was dressed in a coverall garment, so she knew he must be the janitor or night watchman and she relaxed a bit.

"I'm Ayn Remington," she said when he stood in front of her.

His face was stern and he surveyed her from head to toe. Then she saw the worried lines begin to soften. When he spoke again, his words were rushed with excitement, but she understood her name. *"Ayna."* He reached in his back pocket and pulled out a rolled-up pamphlet. Unrolling the curled pages, he showed it to Ayn. Her picture filled the front cover.

She smiled. "Yes, that's me."

He patted her back; then, apparently having second thoughts, he stopped and assumed a sober air. With a bow he removed his cap. When he stood, his face was sheepish. He thrust the program back at her and offered her a pen. She wrote her signature and he beamed with pleasure.

"Your name?" she asked. He didn't understand. She pointed to herself. "I'm Ayn." Pointing to him, she shrugged. On the second try she asked if he was saying Ivan and he nodded. It was at times such as this, alone with one fan, that she remembered why she loved music so much. It broke down all the barriers.

After autographing the program, she indicated she wanted to look around. Ivan nodded and swept his arm wide to show her everything was hers. He retreated backstage after several bows of appreciation.

Ayn stepped up to the podium. Facing where the orchestra should be, she felt eyes gazing upon her. A quick glance over her left shoulder revealed the large portrait of Tchaikovsky looking down on her. His face was so solemn and yet so sensitive. She studied his sorrowful eyes, which had seen so much pain during his lifetime. How incredible that he became the greatest of the Russian composers and the most romantic. In spite of his disastrous marriage, Tchaikovsky trusted in love, and his melodies actually soar with that belief. Ayn looked at him again and wondered if she too would end up a tragic figure in the world of music. Was it her destiny either to enter a doomed marriage or to remain alone forever? Surely there was another choice.

"How did you survive it all and still produce music so far beyond even your own awareness?" she asked his image.

"Ayn," Gerick said, startling her. "What are you doing here?"

She didn't look at Gerick. Her eyes remained on the portrait. "I'm talking to Tchaikovsky, and for a second when you said my name, I thought he was talking back. Now, what are you doing here?"

"I had a few questions for the old boy myself."

She smiled. He never let her get ahead of him. Gerick always had a comeback. "Go on, he's listening."

"So, Peter Ilyitch Tchaikovsky, do you know how treacherous your music is to perform?"

Ayn had hoped that he would pose a question about the two of them, but music was a safer subject. She had to quit living on the false hope that Gerick would change his mind. Trying to act nonchalant, she began chattering. "I think our sad-eyed friend knew all along the predicament he was creating. He's probably laughing at us now. The critics say I have the tendency to milk his work dry. You know, the heart-on-the-sleeve type of thing that leaves the audience racked with inner sobs."

"The critics are right."

Ayn faced him, her hand on her hip. "You don't have to be so quick to agree with them."

"But it's true."

"And what about you? They say you go to the other extreme. When you're forced to play from the Tchaikovsky repertoire you approach it so cautiously that you're in danger of losing the radiance of the music."

"That's true too." He slipped his hands in his coat pocket and rocked on his heels. "Funny, isn't it?"

She wasn't sure where his thoughts were leading. "What's funny?"

"We play our music totally opposite of the way we live our lives. In music I avoid emotion, but I thrive on it in real life. And you, Ayn, are the other way around."

"It's too bad we can't blend our styles and master the best of both worlds."

"Too bad. We'd make quite a team if we could."

They were both talking about more than Tchaikovsky's music, but neither of them had the nerve to pursue it further. Ayn clapped her hands together. "Well, it would have been fun. Now, what are you really doing here?"

"I saw you leave and . . ." He hesitated, then continued telling her that Moscow cabdrivers didn't bring women back into the center of the city.

Disappointment laced her mood. For a brief moment she'd imagined a whole different scene in her mind. She'd seen Gerick begging for her forgiveness and lavishing her with promises of a life together where they'd both be happy. She'd even pictured him saying he loved her so much he couldn't bear another minute apart from her and he would have followed her to the ends of the earth. It was a lovely vision that had shattered as quickly as it had come. Gerick was just being a gentleman, as he would be for any female member of the group.

"Well, I suppose we should be getting back then. I don't want to keep you," she said, marching past him to get her coat.

They each existed in their own thoughts on the

ride back to the National. As they stepped from the cab, Ayn couldn't resist a look toward the citadel. The whole area glowed with the orange-gold lights from the top of Spasskaya Tower. Jonathan's words haunted her. "Will your baton go walking with you in Red Square tonight?" She felt completely alone. Maybe it was the cold air that made her thoughts bitter, but whatever the reason, she felt sad.

Ayn turned back to follow Gerick into the hotel, but found him staring longingly in the same direction as she had been. He was feeling cheated too. Late at night, lovers walked across the square and stole kisses in front of St. Basil's Cathedral. It was the thing to do in Moscow, like a carriage ride through Central Park, a romantic tradition almost as old as the city itself.

"Would you like to walk a little?" Gerick asked. "They say there's nothing more enchanting than Krasnaya Ploshchad at night."

Ayn knew she should say no. Going with him would only be feeding that false hope she kept clinging to. It was a stroll made by lovers, not by two people who had declared their emotions were a lesser need than other forces in their lives. She wanted to be strong and tell him no, then turn and walk away while violins swelled in the background and the camera faded to blackness, but she wasn't a movie star and she wasn't acting from a script. She was a real woman and her heart was breaking and she wanted to be with Gerick.

"Yes," she said as they quietly linked arms. They crossed Marx Prospect and walked down the narrow street between the Historical Museum and the Lenin

Museum. Then, the whole square came into full view.

Ayn drew in her breath. "I didn't expect it to be so pretty."

Gerick patted her hand, which rested on his arm. "Most people think the name Red Square is from the Bolsheviks, but the square was named hundreds of years before the revolution occurred. *Krasnaya* means 'beautiful' as well as 'red.' The literal translation is Beautiful Square."

In every direction Ayn saw couples huddled close as they walked. It was romantic and at the same time, as with so much in Russia, it was practical. Ayn herself snuggled closer to Gerick for warmth. They'd been out long enough that her toes were starting to feel stiff and her cheeks tingled with the cold.

At the cathedral, Ayn couldn't help thinking how it must have been even more impressive when it was built in the sixteenth century.

Gerick dropped his arm to his side, still holding Ayn's hand. "Legend has it that Ivan the Terrible had the architects blinded when the church was finished so they could never build a finer one."

Ayn shivered. "This country has such a cruel and yet romantic history."

He nodded. "If Nicholas had not been so in love with Alexandra that he refused to listen to his people—well, who knows what difference it might have made." He glanced at her sharply. "I used to wonder how his love could have blinded him so much, but I'm beginning to understand how he could forsake an entire nation for one woman."

She looked at him and knew there would never be anyone she would love as totally as she did Gerick. She loved everything about him: the absolutely straight pointedness of his nose, the sensual wave of silver hair at his temple; even his ears seemed perfectly shaped. A smile grew from her childlike adoration.

When he gazed into her eyes, she knew she would carry forever the memory of that one look. For once, she didn't see the color of his eyes, only the need and the love that seemed to extend to a fathomless depth. She felt a quick, painful sadness as she studied the details of his face.

Gerick lifted a trembling hand and brushed back the curly wisps of hair which had escaped from the hood of her coat. He spoke her name with a shudder and kissed her forehead. Though she knew he must be as cold as she was, his lips were warm and they remained touching her gently. When he started to pull away, she tilted her head and stood on her toes to kiss him.

He stiffened. "No, Ayn!" Grasping her shoulders, he forced her away.

She could see the intense blue of his eyes again. They were pleading, but it was a mercy she couldn't grant. Ayn's mind told her to move away, at least to look away, but her heart sent an overture singing out to him through her eyes.

Suddenly he pulled her to him. Rachmaninoff began to play in her head. She wondered if this would be their last kiss. Would it have to sustain her through eternity? The frightening thought drove her into a deeper commitment of giving and sharing.

The kiss became too complete, too fulfilling, and fear finally broke their passion.

Gerick looked as shocked as she did. Then, the tear was there, trickling down her cheek before she realized it existed. It was a final, quiet tear, and it sent her rushing away from him.

Ayn was halfway across the square when her thoughts caught up with her. What am I doing? she asked herself. Only a child runs away from her problems.

He called her name once. Then the bells of the huge clock on the tower began to chime the hour. No, she thought, the only childish thing would be to stay here and pretend there's enough good left between us to work out the bad. She shook her head and hurried on, blinded by her own tears.

Gerick stopped running. He kicked at the snow, sending a fine powder into the frosty air. "That's the last time, Ayn. The very last time I'll give you the chance to walk away from me."

Chapter Ten

The next day was a blur as jet lag began to hit the troupe. Ayn had called a practice, but by midday she dismissed everyone back to their rooms to rest. She retired too, hoping to go over the scores one last time, but soon she gave in to her weariness and slept straight through to the following morning.

The rehearsal on the day of the concert had given way to giddiness and chatter. Ayn was about to let the orchestra go when the main doors opened and closed with a thud. When Ayn heard people walking down the aisle, she wondered why Ivan had not stopped them. She turned to advise whoever it was that no spectators were allowed, but when she saw the intruders, she refrained.

Three official-looking men were walking toward her and a fourth seemed to be guarding the door. Ivan looked very worried and hung his head to keep from looking at Ayn. She knew she'd done nothing wrong, but wondered if one of the orchestra members might have done something without even being aware.

Though he'd been elusive all day, Ayn immediately felt Gerick's presence at her side. She leaned closer to him. "Why do I get the feeling that the Czar has just issued an edict against us?"

Gerick kept his eyes on the approaching visitors. "I'm sure it's nothing."

Before the interruption, Jonathan had been toying at the piano, and in his concentration on the men, his hand fell against the keyboard. The large room vibrated with a C-minor chord. Ayn knew the nervous laughter was due to the fact that the particular key Jonathan had hit was used by Beethoven to connote demons.

The three men lined up in front of her, but Ayn didn't give them time to speak. She offered her hand. "Good afternoon, I'm Ayn Remington, the director. What may I do for you gentlemen?"

The middle man shook her hand; the others did not. "Miss Remington, I'm afraid a matter has come to our attention and the minister of culture requests your presence in his office inside the Kremlin."

The calmness in her voice belied the fear inside her. "May I ask the nature of this matter?"

"I regret I can not divulge that information. Please, come with us now and the minister will explain."

Ayn swallowed. She didn't know what was going on, but she refused to allow her orchestra to sense her insecurity. "Certainly, if I may have a moment to dismiss the players and get my coat?"

The three men agreed in unison and backed up, but they did not sit, indicating they expected her to be prompt. Feeling rebellious, Ayn gave her usual pep talk to the orchestra as she always did before breaking from the final rehearsal. Then she turned with a smile to face the government men. Gerick was already standing with them. He was bundled against the cold and holding her coat. She moved a little steadier knowing that he would be accompanying her.

Jonathan was shoving his arm into his coat sleeve as he came rushing to join them. "I'm going too."

The spokesman for the group nodded to Gerick and Jonathan. "Mr. Eichman and Mr. Grier, the minister requested only to speak with Miss Remington. I assure you she is not in any trouble. This is only a matter of policy to be discussed with the director."

Ayn was relieved at the additional information about the meeting, but she still wanted both of them with her.

"My dear sirs," Jonathan said. "I am conductor laureate of the ISO and I am also serving as official advisor to the orchestra. My advice to the new conductor is not to go unless I am permitted to fulfill my obligation."

The leader looked rather tired as he glanced at his associates. "Very well, Mr. Eichman, you may come along. However, Mr. Grier . . ."

Gerick smiled. "I'm the star." He took Ayn's hand and patted it. With a quick blink he added, "And Miss Remington's fiancé."

Ayn didn't have time to react because Jonathan went into a coughing fit that took all their attention.

When he was finally under control, the official shook his head. "May we proceed now? And yes, you may come also, Mr. Grier."

As they trudged up the aisle, arms linked in Three Musketeer fashion, Ayn threw a sidelong glance at Gerick. "My fiancé?"

"I wanted to be there. It was the only thing I could think of. I could see he wasn't buying the star bit."

Lately, the thought of being engaged or married to Gerick was all she could think about. With the passing of each day the idea seemed more necessary to her happiness, yet at the same time, the consequences seemed more absurd. Hearing Gerick say the words in a lie was devastating.

The air inside the limousine was hot and stale. Ayn found herself thinking of the most unusual things to keep her mind off of her current circumstances. Staring out the window, she couldn't help thinking how different Moscow was from New York. It was a very clean city with no smog, and not once had she seen steam bursting out of a manhole. They were annoying things Ayn never thought she'd miss, but at that moment she'd have given anything to see them. She also wished she could see neon lights and pass by greasy hamburger stands with that delicious fried smell that always made her hungry.

What she missed the most was the lack of noise. Except for minimal traffic sounds, Moscow was a silent city. There were no horns blaring or sirens screaming, not even any police whistles. And the absence of airplanes flying overhead was also disturbing. The one noise she ached to hear right then was the sound of children playing. As they drove through the streets she could see the children now and then, but they never yelled to a friend or laughed aloud. She thought how wonderful it would be to ignore a jeering teenager sitting lazily on a doorstep. Maybe it was her sense of dread that colored the city unjustly now, but she wondered what the world might have missed if Tchaikovsky had been born a hundred years later.

The car stopped and Ayn recognized the Spass-kaya Tower and Gate. After an inspection, the light changed to green and the gate opened. At the gentle click when the iron bars closed behind them, Ayn knew it was time to start worrying.

The corridors were a maze to Ayn after they left the minister's office. She was only half aware of Gerick on one side of her and Jonathan on the other. Her mind kept reliving the scene with the minister. She had prepared herself for several possibilities but not his announcement that no music by an American composer would be allowed at the concert. Ayn had demanded why, but their answer was words that said nothing. Then she tried to convince them they couldn't change selections on her at that point in time. No one cared. It was then she realized the only work on the program by an American was her own symphony.

The knowledge had brought her near tears and she had to stop arguing to contain herself. Above all she could not let them see her break. She vaguely recalled when Jonathan charged that they were being narrow-minded, among other things. His accusations were denied calmly and it became obvious that they'd lost the battle before being shown the enemy.

During the entire session, Gerick had sat quietly

observing. Ayn had thought it would be enough to have him at her side, but as things progressed she found more and more that she wanted him to speak up, to somehow defend her. She'd lost Gerick and she'd lost the premier of her symphony, and very likely, if she'd lost the support of the cultural office, the press would be prejudiced against her too.

That was the final thought that had slipped her into an automated state. She couldn't face it all at once. Slowly, as they walked, she felt herself pulling out of her daze. The world was tuning in again and the pain was almost more than she could bear.

As they started down the outside steps of the Council Building, Ayn squinted at the brightness. Sunlight glinted off the white snow that covered the ground, but especially dazzling was the marble-and-glass Palace of Congress, a building which bore a striking resemblance to Lincoln Center in New York. This time the thought of Manhattan brought no comfort. It only reminded her that she was far away from home and so were many people who were depending on her.

"Oh, Jonathan, what am I going to tell the orchestra?"

"The truth," he said, leading her past the Church of the Twelve Apostles.

"But they've worked so hard to make it perfect for me."

Jonathan patted her hand. "We'll premier the work elsewhere. Right now we need to pull ourselves together. We perform in less than four hours, and tonight, Ayn, we will play the best we have ever played."

Gerick stopped. "Yes, we do need to pull ourselves together. Would you mind if I stayed here awhile and walked around to calm down?"

Ayn wasn't surprised after his apathy inside. She should have suspected he'd pull away from an effort for unity.

"Go on, Gerick, I'll manage fine without you."

Ayn sat in her dressing room watching the clock. As was the custom in Russia, she'd been served her hot tea in a glass and was trying to force it down. The tea wasn't helping; she still couldn't relax. In fact, she couldn't do any of the usual things she did before conducting. All she could think about was how all her dreams had been shattered within a week's time. Often when things seemed the darkest she tried to picture how they would look in a few days. Looked at that way, usually things didn't seem so bad. This time it didn't work. Her world would be just as black and as lonely and as hopeless for a long, long time.

Suddenly the door slammed open. Ayn jumped to her feet, spilling the tea. When she saw it was Gerick, her anger grew. "Look what you made me do!" She grabbed a towel and started wiping the spot she'd made on her dress. "What on earth do you mean barging in here without knocking?"

Gerick looked frantic as he closed the door behind him. "I have to talk to you. It's very important."

Ayn was not in the mood for his dramatics. "Get out!" She stopped trying to wipe the stain from her dress. "I'll talk to you later, after I've changed."

"I'll help you," he said, moving behind her to unzip the white crepe she wore.

"I've had enough of your help already," she said

as the dress fell to her ankles in a pool of ivory. "If you're trying to top a perfectly horrible day, you've succeeded."

"I'm sorry about the dress." He picked it up as she stepped out of the crumple at her feet. Then he draped it over the folding screen as she disappeared behind it. "Ayn, will you listen to me for a minute before they get here?"

She peeked around the screen. "Before who gets here?"

"Never mind just yet. What I have to tell you is that I went back to the minister of culture today after I left you."

"And?"

"And, I have to warn you to go along with whatever they say."

She stepped from behind the screen wearing a black velvet gown. He whistled. "I take back everything I said. I'm not sorry at all for making you change. God, you look even more beautiful in that."

She glanced down. "I'll be hot, but . . ." When she looked up, she noticed for the first time that Gerick also looked beautiful. His tuxedo added class to a man who needed none. She admired the way the suit fit his tall length.

There was a knock at the door. "Please," Gerick pleaded, "go along with them or we may be in big trouble."

"How big?"

"Don't ask."

She nodded. "I've already accepted the fact. You can't fight the government."

He moved to the door and placed his hand on the knob. "There have been some changes since you last talked to them," he whispered. "We might just win after all." Opening the door, he greeted the same men who'd escorted them earlier. "Well, gentlemen, what a surprise to see you here."

The leader stepped forward and gave Gerick a look that said it was no surprise to either of them. "Miss Remington, I am here on behalf of the minister of culture. I am to inform you that your case has been reviewed and the restriction has been lifted."

Ayn blinked in disbelief. "You mean we can premier the symphony tonight?"

"*Da*—yes."

She tried to keep from squealing with delight when she smiled. "How can I ever thank you?"

"Do not thank me. It was due to the additional information provided to our department by your fiancé." The leader then gave an unexpected click of his heels and the three men left the room.

Ayn stared after them, her whole body feeling numb with the news. Slowly, she turned and faced Gerick, tears streaming down her face.

"Good grief, Ayn," he said, rushing to her. "Don't start that now." He took her hand and pulled her to the dressing table. He grabbed a tissue and tried to dry her tears.

"These are tears of joy."

He picked up her baton and placed it in her hand. "Could you be a little less happy so all of Russia doesn't see you red eyed?"

She smiled. "Are we going to end up in Siberia?"

"Only if you trip me up. I told them *The City* was about Moscow."

She broke away from him. "You what?"

"I had to, Ayn; it was the only way."

She backed up and sat in the chair, not trusting her legs to hold her. "But, Gerick, it's so obviously New York."

"To you or me it is, but not to someone who lives here. New York is where everything happens and at such a pace as to inspire greatness. We think of it as the center of the universe. Well, that's exactly how Russians feel about Moscow. *The City* is broad enough to allow the listener to hear what he wants."

She sighed. "Oh, Gerick, what would I ever do without you?"

Ivan peeked in the open door. In a heavily accented voice he announced, "Five minutes, Ayna."

"Spasibo," she answered.

Ivan smiled. "Is good, Ayna, very good."

"I wish I had my lucky basket here to tug on," she said. "I think we're going to need it."

As they stood in the wings, waiting and watching, Gerick's arm arched her waist. The orchestra members took their places and on signal from the first-chair violinist the host announced the orchestra and then introduced Ayn.

Gerick didn't want to let her go from the safety of his arm, but he knew he had to. He released her, and Ayn moved away. Then she stopped and looked back at him as if she wouldn't go without his approval.

"Go for the heart," he encouraged. She winked and took her cue.

As he watched her small figure move to the podium, pride filled him, pride and contentment. She wasn't the same little girl he'd sent off into the world on a winter morning years ago. That Ayn had not looked back, but Ayn Remington, conductor, composer, and woman, looked back. She needed him.

Ayn's symphony ended with what Gerick believed should have had the audience on their feet. She'd built a crescendo so dramatically that his heart wanted to leap from its cavity at hearing the final notes. But the great hall was silent in the rarest of musical phenomena, that silent moment of awe before the full impact hits the listeners. Then the applause thundered their approval and they were on their feet cheering. Even Tchaikovsky seemed to be smiling down at them.

The minute they stepped off the stage, they were each surrounded by fans and well-wishers. In the crush Gerick was separated from Ayn. The crowd continued to grow, overflowing the dressing rooms and spilling into the cavernous backstage area. A half hour passed without Gerick seeing a single face he recognized. When Hank finally appeared and announced the car was ready, Gerick sighed his relief. Normally he enjoyed the adoration of music lovers, but at the moment he only wanted to be with Ayn. He had to talk to her.

He still couldn't locate her outside the auditorium. "Hank," he called. "Where's Ayn?"

Hank cracked his gum. "She went on in one of the other cars."

"To the National?"

"No, the Warsaw. There's a reception in the ballroom."

Gerick sighed.

"The minister of culture arranged it. Everyone is expected to be there," Hank warned, seeing Gerick's irritation.

"Calm down, I'm going." He bent to squeeze into a car full of people he didn't know or care about.

As they drove along the southwest curve of the Garden Ring Road, Gerick wondered if their separation would happen every time they performed together.

From the bridge over the Moscow River, Gerick could see the Moscow State University at Lenin Hills. The "Stalinist Gothic" structure rose thirty-two stories high, the tallest building in the city. Its shape bore a strangely Oriental flavor. He'd wanted to take Ayn up to that hill where Napoleon had first spied the turreted city, but none of his dreams seemed to be coming true.

Gerick looked up. He could see the lights of the Warsaw Hotel just beyond the rim of Gorky Park. "Stop!" he demanded. The driver screeched the wheels to a halt and Gerick climbed out.

One of the passengers rolled down the window. "It's freezing out there. Where are you going?"

Gerick didn't answer. He just continued walking down a frozen path.

Ayn was tired of shaking hands and smiling, but the people kept coming. Then the minister of culture was suddenly in front of her. "Miss Remington, on the behalf of my country I wish to congratulate you. Your performance tonight was quite auspicious and the symphony an ultimate experience."

"Thank you, sir, I—"

"Please." He held up his hand to interrupt. "I also wish to request that your orchestra prolong your stay here beyond the week in Moscow. It is our thought that the peoples of Leningrad and Kiev should hear the music which you've produced. *The City* is a most marvelous tribute to your Russian ancestors."

"Well, I—"

Again he held up his hand. "Then, after touring those cities, we would consider it an honor if you would return to Moscow for our Winter Festival."

"It is you who do us the honor by your invitation," Ayn said, hardly able to contain herself. The festival was considered the epitome of musical excellence. "If our board in New York approves, we accept."

She didn't know Jonathan was near her until he spoke. "They will approve."

The minister smiled. "We will meet in my office tomorrow at three to complete the arrangements." He walked away with his men following him like lost puppies.

Ayn clapped her hands together. "I can't believe it." Suddenly she stopped. "Wait a minute. I don't have any Russian ancestors."

"You do now." Jonathan shrugged. "They had to explain your talent some way."

Ayn laughed, only to sober again. "Jonathan, did you find Gerick?"

"I found something I think you'll like even better."

There was nothing she'd like better than to see Gerick. In spite of everything, she wanted to share the moment with him.

Jonathan took a piece of paper from Hank's hand.

"As you know, the paper won't be out for hours yet, but what I have here is a hand-delivered copy of the review."

A shout went up for silence. Jonathan cracked the paper to attention and cleared his throat. He began to read in Russian. The orchestra booed him and he winked before translating the praise.

Ayn was too excited to focus on every word; only phrases registered.

". . . And as a conductor Miss Remington showed a perfect blend of the elegant style of Mendelssohn and the passionate style of Wagner. . . . As a composer her meanings were infinitely clear. . . . The music seemed to assemble itself over a vast space and the notes spoke of daybreak . . . in *The City*—that same dawn that has magically broken for centuries past and for all the centuries to come. . . . In conclusion, with her work Miss Remington has showed us the hope of new beginnings, which is born with every dawn."

Tears and laughter combined to bubble from her. Jonathan threw his arms around her, his emotions in the same state. A whoopee went up from the orchestra members and champagne corks popped like cannons in the *1812* Overture. The guests broke into another round of applause. Everything would be perfect, Ayn thought, if only Gerick were there.

Before the commotion died, Hank was with them holding Ayn's coat. "What's this for?" she asked.

Jonathan urged her into it. He took her arm and led her out of the ballroom. By the time she'd accompanied him to the outside door of the hotel, Ayn was more than annoyed by his antics. "Jonathan, what's going on? I have hundreds of people waiting for me back there."

"And one out here." He held the door open for her. "The messenger that delivered the review would like to speak with you a moment."

Ayn rolled her eyes. Jonathan took any opportunity to be dramatic. She stood in the doorway looking out. "There's no one here," she said, starting back in. Gently it started, faint at first, then growing louder. It was bells, hundreds of tiny little bells jingling in the frosty night air. Like a vision, the sleigh came down the drive toward the hotel. It was beautiful with a team of three horses pulling it. The silver on their harnesses glittered in the moonlight. Ayn couldn't distinguish the passenger behind the driver, but she knew it was Gerick.

With a spray of snow the sleigh slid to a halt at the front steps. A warmly bundled Gerick stood up. "Your troika awaits, m'lady."

Ayn ran to join him. He helped her climb in, and they huddled close beneath the layers of blankets. There was a crack of the whip and a snort from the lead horse, and they lunged off.

"Now that you're here, this really is the best night of my life." She hugged him. "I owe it all to you for persuading them to let me premier my score."

"Did you think I'd let something as trivial as the Soviet government stand in the way of our love?"

"Then you do still love me?"

"More than ever."

Ayn felt the old fears rising again. "So, where does that leave us?"

"It leaves me with an incredibly large phone bill."

"You mean it's all right for me to travel with the company and we'll keep in touch by telephone?" Somehow that wasn't the solution she'd dreamed of.

"Absolutely not. It means I've already called my agent in New York and tomorrow morning there will be a small news item in the *Times*. It will read something like: 'Violin soloist Gerick Grier announced in Moscow that he will be traveling exclusively with the ISO for the next year and a half. He also revealed that during that period he hopes to collaborate on some classical compositions with his new wife, Ayn Remington, conductor of ISO.'"

"Oh, Gerick, I love you." She began to smother his face with kisses.

"Wait, I'm not through. 'When the newlyweds return to New York they will reside at Mr. Grier's home in the Village. Neighbor Rosy O'Halloran says she's already moved Ms. Remington's lucky basket in and Miss O'Halloran reports that her Benny Goodman collection is awaiting the arrival of the happy couple.'" He took a breath. "I doubt that they're going to print that last part, but I wanted you to know. Do you think we can survive all the changes?"

Ayn's kiss was her answer and she made sure he understood it was yes. She pulled away and smiled. "And after my contract is up with ISO?"

"I thought we'd do guest appearances as a team."

The driver shouted an order to his horses and gently prodded them. The sleigh seemed to fly along the snowscaped trail through Gorky Park. Faster and faster they rode. Delirious with happiness, Ayn let her head fall back and tasted the wind. Above them the crystallized branches of the linden trees twinkled in the moonbeams. The bells jangled, creating a melody.

She laced her gloved fingers with Gerick's. "Do you really want to try writing music too?"

He nodded. "Together I think we can produce the most romantic music the world has ever heard."

She laughed. "Roll over Beethoven, tell Tchaikovsky the news . . ."

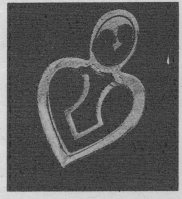

Silhouette Special Edition

MORE ROMANCE FOR
A SPECIAL WAY TO RELAX

$1.95 each

2 ☐ Hastings	21 ☐ Hastings	41 ☐ Halston	60 ☐ Thorne
3 ☐ Dixon	22 ☐ Howard	42 ☐ Drummond	61 ☐ Beckman
4 ☐ Vitek	23 ☐ Charles	43 ☐ Shaw	62 ☐ Bright
5 ☐ Converse	24 ☐ Dixon	44 ☐ Eden	63 ☐ Wallace
6 ☐ Douglass	25 ☐ Hardy	45 ☐ Charles	64 ☐ Converse
7 ☐ Stanford	26 ☐ Scott	46 ☐ Howard	65 ☐ Cates
8 ☐ Halston	27 ☐ Wisdom	47 ☐ Stephens	66 ☐ Mikels
9 ☐ Baxter	28 ☐ Ripy	48 ☐ Ferrell	67 ☐ Shaw
10 ☐ Thiels	29 ☐ Bergen	49 ☐ Hastings	68 ☐ Sinclair
11 ☐ Thornton	30 ☐ Stephens	50 ☐ Browning	69 ☐ Dalton
12 ☐ Sinclair	31 ☐ Baxter	51 ☐ Trent	70 ☐ Clare
13 ☐ Beckman	32 ☐ Douglass	52 ☐ Sinclair	71 ☐ Skillern
14 ☐ Keene	33 ☐ Palmer	53 ☐ Thomas	72 ☐ Belmont
15 ☐ James	35 ☐ James	54 ☐ Hohl	73 ☐ Taylor
16 ☐ Carr	36 ☐ Dailey	55 ☐ Stanford	74 ☐ Wisdom
17 ☐ John	37 ☐ Stanford	56 ☐ Wallace	75 ☐ John
18 ☐ Hamilton	38 ☐ John	57 ☐ Thornton	76 ☐ Ripy
19 ☐ Shaw	39 ☐ Milan	58 ☐ Douglass	77 ☐ Bergen
20 ☐ Musgrave	40 ☐ Converse	59 ☐ Roberts	78 ☐ Gladstone

$2.25 each

79 ☐ Hastings	87 ☐ Dixon	95 ☐ Doyle	103 ☐ Taylor
80 ☐ Douglass	88 ☐ Saxon	96 ☐ Baxter	104 ☐ Wallace
81 ☐ Thornton	89 ☐ Meriwether	97 ☐ Shaw	105 ☐ Sinclair
82 ☐ McKenna	90 ☐ Justin	98 ☐ Hurley	106 ☐ John
83 ☐ Major	91 ☐ Stanford	99 ☐ Dixon	107 ☐ Ross
84 ☐ Stephens	92 ☐ Hamilton	100 ☐ Roberts	108 ☐ Stephens
85 ☐ Beckman	93 ☐ Lacey	101 ☐ Bergen	109 ☐ Beckman
86 ☐ Halston	94 ☐ Barrie	102 ☐ Wallace	110 ☐ Browning

Silhouette Special Edition

$2.25 each

111 ☐ Thorne	133 ☐ Douglass	155 ☐ Lacey	177 ☐ Howard
112 ☐ Belmont	134 ☐ Ripy	156 ☐ Hastings	178 ☐ Bishop
113 ☐ Camp	135 ☐ Seger	157 ☐ Taylor	179 ☐ Meriwether
114 ☐ Ripy	136 ☐ Scott	158 ☐ Charles	180 ☐ Jackson
115 ☐ Halston	137 ☐ Parker	159 ☐ Camp	181 ☐ Browning
116 ☐ Roberts	138 ☐ Thornton	160 ☐ Wisdom	182 ☐ Thornton
117 ☐ Converse	139 ☐ Halston	161 ☐ Stanford	183 ☐ Sinclair
118 ☐ Jackson	140 ☐ Sinclair	162 ☐ Roberts	184 ☐ Daniels
119 ☐ Langan	141 ☐ Saxon	163 ☐ Halston	185 ☐ Gordon
120 ☐ Dixon	142 ☐ Bergen	164 ☐ Ripy	186 ☐ Scott
121 ☐ Shaw	143 ☐ Bright	165 ☐ Lee	
122 ☐ Walker	144 ☐ Meriwether	166 ☐ John	
123 ☐ Douglass	145 ☐ Wallace	167 ☐ Hurley	
124 ☐ Mikels	146 ☐ Thornton	168 ☐ Thornton	
125 ☐ Cates	147 ☐ Dalton	169 ☐ Beckman	
126 ☐ Wildman	148 ☐ Gordon	170 ☐ Paige	
127 ☐ Taylor	149 ☐ Claire	171 ☐ Gray	
128 ☐ Macomber	150 ☐ Dailey	172 ☐ Hamilton	
129 ☐ Rowe	151 ☐ Shaw	173 ☐ Belmont	
130 ☐ Carr	152 ☐ Adams	174 ☐ Dixon	
131 ☐ Lee	153 ☐ Sinclair	175 ☐ Roberts	
132 ☐ Dailey	154 ☐ Malek	176 ☐ Walker	

SILHOUETTE SPECIAL EDITION, Department SE/2
1230 Avenue of the Americas
New York, NY 10020

Please send me the books I have checked above. I am enclosing $_____
(please add 75¢ to cover postage and handling. NYS and NYC residents please
add appropriate sales tax). Send check or money order—no cash or C.O.D.'s
please. Allow six weeks for delivery.

NAME _____

ADDRESS _____

CITY _____ STATE/ZIP _____

Silhouette Special Edition

Coming Next Month

Sea Spell by Abra Taylor

The family curse had warned Danielle that any lover she took
would suffer a terrible misfortune. But when she saw Seth
Whitlaw, she knew that to remain untouched by him would take
all her resolve.

Fit To Be Loved by Antoinette Hardy

Katrina had definitely sworn off all indulgence. Then Fletcher
Ramsey ambled into her health club, and she was sorely tempted
to give in to every whim—especially the romantic sort.

A Song In The Night by Anne Lacey

After Dr. Bryce Emerson, Katie Brentwood had vowed never to
fall for a surgeon again. Then the arrogant doctor came back
into her life, and she knew she was in trouble.

Feathers In The Wind by Margaret Daley

Dr. Kendall Spencer was committed only to her patients. Then
she met Sloan Hunter, and in one shuddering instant she knew
her world had changed utterly.

Business As Usual by Linda Wisdom

As the acting director of Fantasy Toys, Drew faced more than the
usual problems of putting the company back on its feet. Working
under her was Casey McCord, the man she had loved and lost.

For All Time by Sondra Stanford

Lisa Knight expected a hard time getting an interview with
millionaire Anthony Nugent. But the stunning magnetic
attraction of the man took her completely by surprise.